The Case of the Whimsical Weimaraner

A Thousand Islands Doggy Inn Mystery

B.R. Snow

ISBN: 978-1-942691-64-8

Website: www.brsnow.net/
Twitter: @BernSnow
Facebook: facebook.com/bernsnow

Cover Design: Reggie Cullen
Cover Photo: James R. Miller

Other Books by B.R. Snow

The Thousand Islands Doggy Inn Mysteries

The Case of the Abandoned Aussie
The Case of the Brokenhearted Bulldog
The Case of the Caged Cockers
The Case of the Dapper Dandie Dinmont
The Case of the Eccentric Elkhound
The Case of the Faithful Frenchie
The Case of the Graceful Goldens
The Case of the Hurricane Hounds
The Case of the Itinerant Ibizan
The Case of the Jaded Jack Russell
The Case of the Klutz King Charles
The Case of the Lovable Labs
The Case of the Mellow Maltese
The Case of the Natty Newfie
The Case of the Overdue Otterhound
The Case of the Prescient Poodle
The Case of the Quizzical Queens Beagle
The Case of the Reliable Russian Spaniels
The Case of the Salubrious Soft Coated Wheaten
The Case of Italian Indigestion (A Josie and Chef Claire Sojourn)
The Case of the Tenacious Tibetan
The Case of the Unfettered Utonagan
The Case of the Valiant Vizsla

The Whiskey Run Chronicles

The Whiskey Run Chronicles – The Complete Volume 1
The Whiskey Run Chronicles – The Complete Volume 2

Doc White Adventures

Getting Greedy

The Damaged Posse

American Midnight
Larrikin Gene
Sneaker World
Summerman
The Duplicates

Other Books

Divorce Hotel
Either Ore
Get Off Your Duff and Write the Book

To Apple and John

Chapter 1

Of all the murderous thoughts I've had over the past few months, and there have been many, I'd put this one near the top of the list. And if forced to spend ten more minutes dealing with sweat pouring into my eyes and three inches of soft sand sucking at the bottom of my feet, this particular experience would rocket to the top of the charts with a bullet. I glared at Chef Claire who, as always, was churning along the beach barely breaking a sweat. She knew I was giving her my best death stare, although she avoided eye contact as she continued her effortless stride.

"Keep going. You're doing great."

"Shut it."

"Fine," she said, still not making eye contact. "Be miserable."

"What choice do I have?"

"You always have a choice."

"Then I'm gonna go with miserable."

"Don't forget whiny and petulant."

"You're repeating yourself," I said, fighting off a stitch emerging from the bottom of my ribcage. "They're synonyms."

"They are?" she said, glancing over.

"Yeah," I whispered as I returned her stare through bared teeth.

"Are you sure?"

"Who the hell cares?" I said, maintaining my glare.

"Well, then I guess it bears repeating," she said, then laughed.

"I hate you."

"Tell me something I don't know," Chef Claire said, picking up the pace. "C'mon, slacker. Move it."

"We should turn around and head back," I said, glancing over my shoulder. "Max needs me."

"Max is in the pool with your mom and Josie," Chef Claire said. "She probably doesn't even realize you're not there."

"Gee, thanks, Chef Claire. That makes me feel so much better."

"Glad I could help."

"I hate you."

"Now who's repeating herself?"

I gnawed on my bottom lip as I glanced out at the water. The sun was making its way into midday position, and I felt rivulets of sweat trailing down my spine. The sand did its best to rip my running shoes off my feet as I forced myself to keep churning forward. In the distance, I spotted the beginning of the resorts that covered a long stretch of Seven Mile Beach and a small smile emerged.

"Okay, I see the hotels," I said. "We can turn around now."

"Another quarter-mile," Chef Claire said.

"Ugh."

Mercifully, a few minutes later, Chef Claire came to a stop and placed her hands on her hips as she stared out at the calm sea. Bent over at the waist, I sucked air, oblivious to my placid surroundings.

"It's a beautiful morning," Chef Claire said, her breathing already back to normal.

"We must have a different definition," I said with a grimace as I clutched my side. "Have you got your phone with you?"

"I do. Why?"

"I think I'll catch a cab back to the house," I said.

"Suzy, we've gone a mile and a half," Chef Claire said, staring at me in disbelief.

"What's your point?"

"Unbelievable. Just take a few minutes to catch your breath and you'll be fine."

"Easy for you to say," I said.

"Complain all you want," Chef Claire said. "But in case you haven't noticed, this exercise program happens to be working."

"It is?" I said with a frown.

"Have you weighed yourself lately?"

"No. I have an agreement with my scale. I don't stand on it, and it doesn't ruin my day."

"You must have dropped five pounds. Maybe even ten."

"No way," I said.

"How could you not know that?"

"Really?"

"Absolutely. You look great," Chef Claire said. "You haven't noticed your clothes getting looser?"

"I wear drawstring shorts and tee shirts," I said, shrugging. "And I guess between taking care of Max and figuring out ways to kill you without getting caught for putting me through this torture, it slipped my mind."

"Well, you can thank me now," Chef Claire said with a grin.

"Let's not get ahead of ourselves," I said, gently punching her on the shoulder.

"There's my girl. Okay, let's head back," she said, pointing in the direction of the house. "I'm hungry."

"How can you even think of food at a time like this?"

Chef Claire reached out and placed a hand on my forehead.

"What are you doing?" I said.

"Just checking to make sure you're not running a fever," she said.

"Funny," I said, following her lead and breaking into a slow trot back down the beach.

As I ran, I replayed Chef Claire's comment about my weight loss. Maybe it was time to revisit my agreement with the bathroom scale. I gently pinched the skin at the top of my shorts and grunted with surprise at the lack of a muffin top.

"Son of a gun," I whispered.

"What's that?" Chef Claire said, glancing over.

"I think you're right," I said. "I'm losing weight."

"Told ya," she said, laughing. "Maybe you'll stop whining every morning when we go for our run."

"Oh, I don't like your chances," I said, again fighting back against the stitch in my side.

We continued our trek down the beach then both slowed at the same time.

"Is that what I think it is?" I said.

"I'm afraid so," Chef Claire said. "Let's hope it's just a drunk tourist."

We broke into a run and soon found ourselves staring down at a middle-aged man lying on his side. He was drenched and covered in sand. We dropped to our knees, and Chef Claire gently pressed two fingers against his neck to check for a pulse.

"Are you getting anything?" I said, glancing up and down the man's body for signs of injuries.

"Barely," she said, reaching for her phone.

I dropped to my knees and checked to make sure nothing was obstructing his breathing. I began applying a series of check compressions, followed by a few short breaths. He remained unresponsive.

"Geez, the poor guy," I whispered, glancing up at her. "How the heck did he get here?"

"I'm gonna guess the ocean," Chef Claire deadpanned.

"Thanks for clarifying," I said, frowning at her as I began another round of chest compressions. "What I mean is, how did he end up on the beach? We just ran by this spot ten minutes ago."

"I don't have a clue," she said, waiting for the call to connect. "It's certainly odd."

I continued administering CPR as I listened to her side of the conversation. When the call ended, she slipped her phone into her shorts and sat down next to me in the sand.

"They're on their way," Chef Claire said. "Is there anything else we can do for him while we wait?"

"I guess a little prayer couldn't hurt," I said, staring at the lifeless body that seemed to have appeared out of thin air.

Chapter 2

We watched Detective Renfro rapidly make his way across the sand. He spotted us and gave us a small wave as he continued the short trek. Chef Claire knelt next to me and took a turn administering CPR.

"He looks tired," I said, studying the detective movements.

"He and his wife were at the restaurant the other night," Chef Claire said. "They're both exhausted. Like they've been run over by a truck. They had twins."

"I know," I said. "They must be walking by now, right?"

"No, they just had another set of twins."

"You're kidding."

"Apparently twins run in both sides of their families," she said.

"Geez. I can't even imagine."

"What? Having four of Max?" she said, then resumed counting the chest compressions.

"Perish the thought," I said, then waved at Detective Renfro. "Good morning, Detective."

"Hi, Suzy. Chef Claire," the detective said, shaking hands with both of us. "Great dinner the other night. We really needed a night out."

"I bet you did," Chef Claire said.

"Congratulations on the new arrivals," I said.

"Thanks," the detective said, stifling a yawn. "They're a handful. What have we got here?"

"We were jogging and spotted him on the way back to the house."

Detective Renfro knelt down in the sand and slipped on a pair of latex gloves. Chef Claire stopped her work and slid to the side to give him room. He checked for signs of a pulse.

"Are you getting anything?" Chef Claire said.

"It's really weak," he said. "And fading fast, I'm afraid."

"Should I keep going?"

"It probably couldn't hurt," the detective said. "Apart from the CPR, did you move the body?"

"What am I, an amateur?"

"I was just about to say that I've missed you, Suzy," Detective Renfro whispered without looking up.

"What?" I said.

"Nothing," he said, patting the man's shorts then removing a plastic bag from one of the pockets.

"What's that?" I said, immediately on point.

Detective Renfro began removing items from the bag.

"California driver's license, social security card."

"He's American?" I said, reading over the detective's shoulder.

"Nothing gets past you," Chef Claire said, shaking her head as she continued applying chest compressions.

"I don't think I'm talking to you," I said.

"Really? Tell me how I did it so I can make it happen again," Chef Claire said.

"Here's a photocopy of his passport information," Detective Renfro said, unfazed by our banter.

"Photocopy?" I said. "Why would he have a photocopy?"

"A lot of people don't like carrying their passport around," he said.

"I guess that makes sense," I said with a shrug.

"William Quiver?" Detective Renfro said. "Why does that name sound familiar?"

Chef Claire and I glanced at each other then shrugged.

"I know I've heard that name before," he said. "What's keeping that ambulance?"

"What's that?" I said, nodding at a folded piece of paper still inside the plastic bag.

Detective Renfro removed the paper and studied it before holding it out so I could read it.

"A suicide note?" I said, glancing back and forth at them. "That's weird."

"Why do you say that?" Detective Renfro said.

"Who commits suicide on the beach?" I said.

"What?" Chef Claire said, frowning at me.

"I mean the guy had a whole ocean out there," I said.

"Well, he's soaked," Chef Claire said. "Maybe he jumped in and changed his mind. You know, he panicked and tried to swim to shore."

"Maybe," I said, giving it some thought.

"That's not a bad theory, Chef Claire," Detective Renfro said.

"I guess living with her does have some benefits," she said, without looking up. "Eventually, some of it has to rub off, right?"

"I'm gonna take that as a compliment," I said, trying to read the note over the detective's shoulder. "What did he have to say for himself?"

"There's just a comment about how it's not worth it. Something about too many prying eyes."

"He must have been in some sort of trouble," I said. "There's a PS at the bottom of the note. What does it say?"

"Take good care of Ruby," Detective Renfro said.

"Wife? Daughter? Maybe his girlfriend?" I said.

The detective shrugged, refolded the note and slipped it back in the bag along with the other items. He slid it into his shirt pocket and glanced out at the water. My eyes followed his, and we both settled on a powerboat anchored a few hundred feet offshore.

"You think that might be his boat?" I said.

"Could be," he said. "Did you notice if it was there when you ran by this section of beach?"

"I was preoccupied at the time," I said.

"With what?" Detective Renfro said.

"Survival."

"I never would have pegged you as a jogger," he said.

"Trust me, it's not by choice," I said, shooting Chef Claire a dirty look before glancing down at the man in the sand. "Something about this doesn't make sense."

"Don't start, Suzy," Chef Claire said.

"What?" I said.

"You know what I'm talking about. You've got that look."

"I'm just saying it doesn't make sense. Unless your theory about him having a change of heart is right."

"You got a better theory?" Chef Claire said.

"No. Not yet."

"Do you know who that is?" she said, spotting a woman sprinting across the sand toward us.

"Oh, that's Samantha," Detective Renfro said as he waved to her. "She's down here for a month while Jimmy is away."

"Where's Jimmy?" I said.

"Vacation," Detective Renfro said. "And I think he's doing some interviews while he's back in the States."

"He wants to leave Cayman?" I said, surprised by the news.

"Yeah, he's bored being a medical officer down here," Detective Renfro said. "Not enough action for him."

"His timing is great," I said. "He leaves the island, and somebody turns up dead as soon as he's gone."

"Yeah, the guy can't catch a break," Detective Renfro said, then frowned. "Sorry. That didn't come out right."

The medical officer named Samantha arrived and immediately knelt down to examine the body. A few moments later, she got to her feet and shook her head as she blinked back tears.

"He's gone," she whispered.

"Did you know him?" I said, puzzled by her tears.

"What?" Samantha said.

"You're crying," I said.

"Oh, that," she said, waving it off. "I always cry when I see a dead body. It's something I thought I'd eventually outgrow, but it never happened."

"Occupational hazard," I said, then smiled at her and extended my hand. "I'm Suzy."

"Samantha," she said, returning the handshake. "Samantha Powers. How are you, Detective Renfro?"

"I'm good," the detective said. "Your second day here and already right in the middle of things, huh?"

"Yeah," she said, glancing down at the body. "Jimmy swore I'd spend the month sitting at my desk reading magazines."

"You got here fast," Detective Renfro said. "You even beat the ambulance."

"I was having breakfast at that café you recommended," Samantha said. "I heard the chatter on the radio." She glanced down at the body again. "Who's the victim?"

"His name is William Quiver," the detective said. "The name sounds familiar, but I don't have a clue why."

"I'm sorry," Samantha said, her eyes landing on Chef Claire. "Where are my manners?" She extended her hand. "I'm Samantha Powers."

"Nice to meet you. I'm Chef Claire."

"I know you," Samantha said. "From the restaurant. I saw you there last night. That was you, right?"

"That was me," Chef Claire said.

"Jimmy told me the first thing I needed to do when I got here was to have dinner there. It was fantastic."

"Thanks. We try to do our best," Chef Claire said.

"And it's your restaurant?" Samantha said.

"Four of us own it," Chef Claire said, nodding at me. "Suzy and her mom. And our other friend, Josie."

"I had the crab curry," Samantha said. "It was unbelievable."

All of us spotted two paramedics trotting across the sand. Samantha remained focused on them until they arrived.

"Morning," one of the paramedics said, glancing around at all of us. "What have we got?"

"Looks like a suicide," Detective Renfro said.

"He's gone," Samantha said. "There's no need to rush. And just take him straight to the morgue."

"Got it," the paramedic said.

We watched in silence as they went to work.

"Where are you staying while you're here?" I said.

"At Jimmy's place," Samantha said, keeping a close eye on the paramedics.

"This is the first time you've been to Cayman?" I said.

"It is," she said. "I don't know a soul. Well, apart from you guys."

"We can fix that," I said. "We're having a barbeque at our place tonight. Why don't you come?"

"That sounds like fun," Samantha said.

"Great. Our place is the big white one with all the glass. It's about a mile up the beach from here," I said, pointing. "Anytime around seven."

"Thank you. What can I bring?"

"Just yourself and your appetite," Chef Claire said.

"I'll be there," she said, then she cocked her head. "You wouldn't happen to have any suggestions about where I might get a dog?"

"I could probably ballpark it," I said, laughing.

"What?"

"We run a rescue shelter on the island," I said.

"Your life centers around food and dogs?" Samantha said.

"Yeah, pretty much," I said, nodding.

"I want your life," she said.

"Be careful what you wish for," Chef Claire deadpanned.

"Shut it," I said, frowning at her before turning back to Samantha. "You want to get a dog?"

"I do," she said. "I have a feeling I'm going to be here for a while. Jimmy's positive he's going to get several job offers over the next month. Two things I've always wanted to do are to live on a tropical island and get a dog. A big dog."

"We can certainly help you with that," I said. "Actually, the woman who manages our shelter will be at the barbeque. She'll be happy to answer all your questions."

"Well, apart from the dead body on the beach," Samantha said. "I have to say this has turned out to be a productive morning."

"How about you, Detective Renfro?" Chef Claire said. "Can you make it to the party tonight?"

"I'd love to," he said. "But the older twins are fighting colds. So, we better stay close to home tonight."

"The poor little guys," I said. "Maybe you can make the next one."

"Sounds great," he said, watching as the paramedics began carrying the body across the sand. "Okay, we're done here. I need to run. I've got a ton of paperwork to process on this one. See you guys soon. If you need anything, Samantha, you know where to find me."

"Will do," she said. "I need to follow the paramedics. See you tonight."

"Come hungry," Chef Claire said.

Samantha gave us a wave and followed Detective Renfro as he trudged through the sand.

"She seems nice," Chef Claire said.

"She does," I said. "An eater who likes dogs. How bad can she be, right?"

Chef Claire laughed and arched her back to stretch.

"You ready?"

"I thought we'd walk back," I said.

"Why?"

"I'm traumatized," I said, glancing over at her. "Finding a dead body in the sand and all that."

"Yeah, you look positively devastated," she said, shaking her head.

"I'm hiding it. You know, burying my true feelings about this tragic event."

"Stuff a sock in it, Suzy. Let's go. I'll race you back to the house."

"Not gonna happen," I said, beginning a leisurely stroll.

"You're really gonna use this as an excuse?"

"Unless you've got a better one," I said, beaming at her.

Chapter 3

As we neared the path that led up to the house, something in the distance again caught our eye. But instead of being sprawled out face down in the sand, this particular object of interest was very much alive and bouncing up and down on its front paws at the water's edge.

"What on earth is she doing?" Chef Claire said, laughing as we watched the dog.

"I have no idea," I said, laughing along. "She's gorgeous."

"Weimaraner, right?"

"Yeah. But I don't see anybody around," I said. "I hope she's not lost."

We changed direction and headed toward the water. When we were about a hundred feet away, I whistled softly, and the dog cocked her head then dashed toward us. I leaned down to greet her, but the dog began to circle both of us at a frenetic pace. After completing several laps, the dog sat down on her haunches and stared at us. I took a step forward to pet her, but the dog playfully scooted back a few feet just out of reach. I took another step and the dog hopped to all fours and resumed her circling. Chef Claire and I laughed as we watched the dog begin to create what looked like a small racetrack oval in the sand.

Eventually, the dog either got tired or dizzy and sat back down and stared at us.

"What a goofball," I said, still laughing.

"She's a beautiful dog," Chef Claire said. "What color are her eyes?"

"Greenish-brown, I think. Weimaraners are usually born with bright blue eyes, but they start to change color around six months."

"How old do you think she is?" Chef Claire said, extending a hand toward the dog.

"She can't be more than a year or two," I said, also reaching out to pet the dog. "I love that silver coat."

"Sleek," Chef Claire said.

"Good word. Let's see if she's got a name tag on that collar."

I sat down on my knees and slowly leaned forward. This time, the dog inched closer to me and accepted the gentle ear scratch I gave her. She was panting heavily.

"She's been out in the sun for a while," I said, now using both hands to rub the dog's head. "We need to get her up to the house and give her some water."

Chef Claire slid closer and gently slid her hand down the dog's back. The Weimaraner's tail began wagging furiously.

"Oh, you like that, huh?" Chef Claire said, then reached for the dog's collar. She read the name tag then grunted. "How about that?'

"What is it?" I said, glancing over at her.

"Her name is Ruby."

"Take good care of Ruby," I said, remembering the postscript on the suicide note. "Son of a gun." I sat down in the sand, my mind racing. "Give Josie a call and have her head down here with a leash."

"Good idea," she said, digging her phone out of her shorts. "And you said your brain shuts down after exercise."

"The walk cleared my mind," I said.

"Yeah, that must be it," she deadpanned, then spoke into the phone. "Hey…No, everything's good…A bit whiny but not bad today."

"Hey," I said, glaring at her as I held onto the dog's collar.

"We just came across the most gorgeous Weimaraner you've ever seen…Geez, Josie. I know you haven't seen her yet. It's a figure of speech. We need you to head down the beach and bring a leash with you…I'll tell you all about it when you get here. Thanks." She put her phone away and shook her head. "Everybody's a comedian."

The dog sat quietly in the sand and glanced back and forth at us. She continued to pant and her tongue hung from one side of her mouth. Moments later, we heard the gate open and Josie came into view. The dog got to her feet and pulled back against my grip.

"She's strong," I said, holding on tight. "Good girl, Ruby. There you go. Good girl."

Josie knelt down next to the dog and patted her head with one hand and attached the lead with the other.

"You weren't kidding," Josie said, admiring the dog. "She's beautiful. You found her here on the beach?"

"Right after we found her owner face down in the sand," I said.

"Drunk?"

"Dead," I said, climbing to my feet.

"What?"

"Yeah, he committed suicide," Chef Claire said. "Long story."

"I'll make time," Josie said. "She's thirsty. Let's get her up to the house."

We headed up the path, and as soon as the gate was closed behind us, Josie removed the leash. We watched the Weimaraner's reaction to her new surroundings. Whatever initial impressions she may have had were cut short when the four house dogs, who'd been fighting over a toy in the pool, spotted the interloper. All four clamored out of the water, shook torrents of water off them, then made a beeline for Ruby. The Weimaraner met them halfway across the lawn, and all five dogs spent time checking each other out. But as always, the house dogs were unfazed by the new arrival. Captain, Josie's Newfie, confirmed their acceptance with a gentle nudge of his head against Ruby's, then led the parade back into the pool. Soon, all five were roughhousing in the water.

"Unbelievable," Josie said, watching the dogs play. "We humanoids could learn a few things from them about acceptance."

"Well, they do spend most of their time back home surrounded by seventy other dogs. What's one more, right?"

"Yeah," Josie said. "But still, they're amazing creatures."

"I'll get her some water," Chef Claire said, heading for the outside tap.

When I reached the back patio, about twenty degrees cooler due to the awning and overhead misting system that was working overtime, Max spotted me. Perched on my mother's lap, she giggled, kicked her legs and held out her arms. Overwhelmed with emotion, as I always was whenever she gave me the pick-me-up signal, I gently lifted her into my arms.

"And how are you?" I cooed.

"She's wonderful," my mother said. "I got her out of the pool about a half-hour ago. It's too hot out there."

"Good call, Mom," I said, bending down to kiss her cheek. "Hey, Paulie. How are you doing today?"

"Couldn't be better," he said from the comfort of a lounge chair. "Your mother and I were just deciding how we were going to spend the day."

"And?" I said, glancing back and forth at them.

"This is as far as we got," Paulie said, laughing.

"I'm very content right here," my mother said. "That's a beautiful dog, darling. Was she running loose on the beach?"

"She was," I said.

"I knew a guy in Rochester whose kid bred Weimaraners," Paulie said. "He loved that breed."

"Rochester?" I said, grinning at him. "Back during your somewhat darker days as a criminal?"

"Vicious and unfounded rumors," he said, grinning back.

"Please, don't start, darling," my mother said, reaching out to take Max back. "Come to Grandma."

"The old man was a piece of work," Paulie said, drifting off momentarily on a memory. "Slash was something else."

"Slash?" I said, sitting down. "As in, he was a fan of cutlery?"

"He loved it," Paulie said, nodding.

"I take it he wasn't a chef," I said.

"No, most of Slash's…carving was done on…let's call them inedible creatures."

"Yuk," I said, scowling at him. "Geez, Paulie. Must you?"

"I could be a lot more graphic if you like."

"No, that's okay," I said. "I get the point."

"I wonder what happened to his kid. I haven't seen him in over twenty years. Last I heard, he decided he couldn't take another winter and moved to California."

At the mention of California, a couple of neurons collided and I scowled.

"What's the matter?" Paulie said.

"Nothing," I said, shaking my head. "That's just the second California reference I've heard this morning."

"Yeah, old Slash was something else," Paulie said with a chuckle.

"Was? What happened to him?" I said.

"He eventually got a taste of his own medicine. Should I be more descriptive?"

"No, thanks. I got it."

"Slash Quiver," Paulie said, shaking his head. "I haven't thought about him in years. A lot of memories. And most of them bad."

"Slash *Quiver*?"

"Yeah," Paulie said. "Weird name, huh?"

"His kid didn't happen to be called William by any chance?"

"How the hell did you know that?"

"We just met him on the beach," I said, rubbing my forehead.

"What?"

"Yeah," I whispered.

"What did he have to say for himself?" Paulie said.

"He was pretty quiet," I said, gnawing on my bottom lip.

"Yeah, I remember," Paulie said, nodding. "The kid pretty much kept to himself. Spent most of the time with his dogs."

"He's dead," I said softly.

"Dead?" Paulie said, stunned by the news.

"What happened to him, darling?"

"Suicide. He left a note. That's how we know the Weimaraner was his dog."

"Suicide? Little Billy Quiver?" Paulie said, shaking his head. "Not a chance."

"Why do you say that?" I said.

"Because I knew the family very well," Paulie said. "There's no way he killed himself. Especially if he still had one of those dogs." He shook his head. "Not a chance."

"But the note said it wasn't worth it, and there were too many prying eyes."

"I don't care what the note says," Paulie said. "The guy didn't kill himself."

"You said you hadn't seen him in over twenty years," I said, protesting. "That's a long time. And people change."

"The Quivers come from a strict Orthodox religion," Paulie said. "I don't know what sort of trouble he was in, but there's no way Little Billy would have done that."

"Was he involved in any sort of criminal activities?"

"He was a Quiver," Paulie said with a shrug. "Of course, he was a criminal."

"Doing what?"

"Anything his father told him to do. Except for the carving. Slash refused to delegate that one."

"Geez, Paulie," I said, frowning at him again. "Must you?"

"When did you turn squeamish?"

"I'm not squeamish. We're talking about the kid. What sort of stuff was the family involved in?"

"Well, Little Billy's grandfather was a bootlegger during Prohibition and made a fortune. Then Slash got into running drugs in the Seventies and made another fortune. I imagine Billy inherited it all when his dad died."

"When was that?" I said, trying to select from the plethora of questions now rolling around my head.

"It must have been soon after Little Billy moved to California," Paulie said. "I never really paid much attention. I was out of the game by then."

"Are there other family members still around?"

"I don't think so. Maybe some cousins, but that would be it. All the people from his dad's generation are all gone."

"Ooh," my mother said, getting to her feet. "Somebody needs a change."

"I'll take care of it, Mom," I said.

"No, you just sit there and keep tormenting Paulie," she said.

"I'm not tormenting him," I said. "We're just chatting."

"Of course," she said, gently jiggling Max in her arms. "Should I get her down for a nap?"

"Yeah, that's probably a good idea," I said, gently running a hand over Max's cheek. "Thanks, Mom."

She headed inside the house, and I refocused on Paulie who was deep in thought.

"If you're right and it wasn't a suicide, that means somebody killed him," I said, staring out at the pool where the dogs had Josie and Chef Claire surrounded.

"Is this the part where I'm supposed to say nothing gets past you?" Paulie said, laughing.

"Shut it."

Chapter 4

The smells wafting in the breeze took my hunger to a whole new level. I studied Paulie and my mom as they worked in tandem, coordinating several different types of meat and fish on the enormous grill.

"It almost looks like they're performing a synchronized dance routine," Josie said with a laugh.

"Yeah, they're quite the pair," I said, smiling as I watched my mother flip a steak and take a sip of wine without interrupting the conversation she was having with her constant companion.

"You think they'll ever make it official?" Chef Claire said. "You know, tie the knot?"

"I doubt it," I said, shaking my head. "They both say they don't want to do anything that might mess it up."

"Makes sense," Josie said. "Why take the risk, huh? It smells fantastic. A couple of those steaks have my name on them."

"A couple?" Chef Claire said with a frown. "Have you seen the size of those things?"

"What's your point?" Josie said, then reached out to take Max. "Come here, you."

"I love those pajamas," Chef Claire said, laughing. "Where on earth did you find them?"

"Online," Josie said as she continued holding her arms out. "Every kid should have a pair of pajamas with dogs on them."

Max extended her arms and Josie gently held her against her chest. Max glanced back and forth at the guests who were scattered in small groups near the pool and at various tables set up on the lawn. Then she focused on me and yawned.

"Somebody's tired," I said.

"She spent most of the day playing with the dogs," Chef Claire said. "She's worn out."

"You want me to see if she'll go down for a nap?" Josie said.

"You can try," I said. "But if she won't, just bring her back out."

"I'll be right back," Josie said, then headed for the house.

We watched her depart with Max, then Chef Claire turned to me.

"Paulie's convinced the guy didn't kill himself?"

"He is," I said. "I'm having a hard time believing it."

"Me too. If somebody did kill him, they only had ten minutes to pull it off. We'd just run by that stretch of sand."

"Yeah, that part has been driving me nuts all afternoon," I said, rubbing my forehead.

"Now, there's a surprise," Chef Claire said with a laugh.

"Funny," I said, making a face at her before brightening when I spotted someone heading our way. "Here comes the Premier."

Gerald slowly worked his way through the crowd, pausing to chat briefly with several guests. He waved to my mother and Paulie before giving both of us a long hug.

"Good evening, Gerald," I said. "How goes the battle of running the affairs of state?"

"To tell you the truth, Suzy, I've had better days," he said softly.

"What's the matter?" Chef Claire said.

"I got some distressing news today," he said. "Someone I knew died."

"William Quiver?" I said.

"Word travels fast," Gerald said.

"We're the ones that found the body," I said.

"Really? On the beach?"

"We were out for our morning run," Chef Claire said.

"Was he a friend of yours?" I said.

"More of a business acquaintance," Gerald said, not making eye contact.

"What kind of business?" I said, raising an eyebrow.

"It was of the *none of your* variety," Gerald said, giving me a playful grin.

"Everybody's a comedian," I said. "Paulie's convinced it wasn't a suicide."

"Paulie?" Gerald said, surprised. "Why on earth would he have an opinion on the matter?"

"He knew him," I said. "Paulie used to cross paths with William's old man."

"Yes, Slash," Gerald said, nodding. "A despicable human being."

"You knew his father?" I said.

"I met him a few times," Gerald said, again glancing off into the distance. "A long time ago."

"When was that?" I said.

"Suzy, I get fewer questions at one of my cabinet meetings," he said, shaking his head.

"Why do I get the feeling you're hiding something, Gerald?" I said, then glanced at Chef Claire. "Are you getting the same vibe?"

"Oh, I'm going to sit this one out," Chef Claire said. "But keep going. This could get interesting."

"You're no help," Gerald said.

"You met Slash Quiver before you got into politics?"

"Yes," Gerald said softly.

"Back when you were still in the…now, what should we call it...the *finance* industry?"

"Isn't dinner ready yet?" Gerald said, glancing at the grill.

I rubbed my forehead, deep in thought, then snapped my fingers when the penny dropped.

"Slash Quiver came down here after he got into the heroin business, didn't he?" I said. "Son of a gun. You helped the guy launder his drug money. That's it, isn't it?"

"How on earth do you do that?" Gerald said, staring at me in disbelief.

"Do what?"

"Put all that together from a couple of tidbits?"

"I'm in touch with the universe," I deadpanned, then turned serious. "I'm right, aren't I?"

"Perhaps."

"How could you do something like that, Gerald?" I said through narrowed eyes.

"While I may have helped him put together a structure for his…banking needs, I had no idea how he made his money."

"Really?" I said, raising an eyebrow again.

"I may have had my suspicions," he said with a shrug. "But it was none of my business. And it was back in the day when things were handled more loosely than they are now. We've tightened things up a lot."

"Don't you mean you've tightened things up because there are a lot more people keeping a close eye on how you guys do things down here?" I said.

"Tomato, tomahto," Gerald said.

"Geez," I said, shaking my head. "Laundering money for a heroin dealer. That probably wouldn't be good information to have floating around the general public."

"Suzy, please," he said. "Ancient history."

"What about the son?" I said.

"What about him?"

"Did he have a place down here?"

"I believe he did," Gerald said. "But I only know that through secondhand information."

"You weren't doing business with him?" I said.

"Suzy, I'm the Premier down here. I run the government," Gerald snapped. "And my deepest desire is to keep running the government. So, can we please drop the subject?"

"I touched a nerve," I said, glancing at Chef Claire.

"You certainly did," she said, studying the Premier's expression. "What's going on, Gerald?"

He stared across the lawn and exhaled loudly.

"I received an anonymous letter the other day."

"Here we go," I said. "What did it say?"

"It made some references to how it was time for me to be held accountable for my past actions."

"Blackmail?" I said.

"No, it was more of a threat to my personal safety," Gerald said.

"Do you think William Quiver had anything to do with it?" I said.

"At the time, I had no idea who sent it," he said. "Now, I'm sure it was Little Billy."

"Why would he threaten you?" Chef Claire said.

Gerald didn't respond. I let my neurons work their magic, then another penny landed with a thud.

"You did something to his old man, didn't you?" I said.

"Unbelievable," Gerald whispered.

"You did something to, or with his money, right?"

"I may have," he said. "It's really not important, Suzy. Like I said, it's ancient history."

"Like that's gonna stop her," Chef Claire said with a laugh. "What did you do, Gerald?" she said in a singsong voice.

"I really don't want to talk about it."

"Holy crap," I whispered, then stared at the Premier. "You were worried your political career would never get off the ground if word got out you had helped the old man launder drug money."

"And to think I turned down a chance to have dinner with a visiting dignitary tonight," Gerald said, scratching his head.

"So, you sold the guy out, then probably leaked something to the press about how you had discovered the guy was running heroin and turned yourself into a local hero," I said. "What a great way to launch your political career. That was frigging genius, Gerald."

"Thanks," he whispered. "But that's not what happened."

"Did you have the old man arrested?" Chef Claire said.

"No," he said, shaking his head.

"You had his accounts frozen, right?" I said.

"Yes, I spoke with a few colleagues who worked for the government at the time."

"Such a cozy relationship you guys have down here," I said, laughing. "How much money are we talking about?"

"A little over fifty million," Gerald said.

"Geez," I grunted. "And William just started asking for it back? Why did he wait so long?"

"I have no idea. My best guess is he never knew his father had an account down here."

"So, he somehow learned about the money then showed up at the bank and was told the account was frozen," I said.

"Something like that, yes," Gerald said.

"And he managed to piece together what happened?" I said.

"Again, that would be my best guess."

"Your name came up during his search. Then the anonymous letter showed up at your office," I said.

"That pretty much sums it up," he said.

"I'd love to see that letter."

"Swing by my office," he said, then gave me a playful grin.

"Your office?" I said, frowning. "I don't know, Gerald."

"Just try to keep your clothes on this time," Chef Claire said with a laugh.

"Shut it," I said, glaring at her before focusing on Gerald. "If it was a suicide, your problem goes away."

"I must admit the thought has crossed my mind," he said.

"But if the guy was murdered, that's a potential gamechanger," I said.

"How so?" Chef Claire said.

"Because of the motive."

"Motive?"

"Yeah," I said with a nod.

"Whose motive?" Chef Claire said.

"His," I said, pointing at Gerald.

"Mine?"

"Yeah, I think somebody might be trying to set you up for murder, Gerald," I said, giving the idea some serious thought.

"But Little Billy is dead," Chef Claire said. "Who else would want to set Gerald up?"

"I don't have a clue," I said, shrugging. "Yet."

"You don't have a clue about what?" Josie said, returning empty-handed.

"Who might be setting Gerald up for murder," Chef Claire said.

"Interesting," Josie said, nodding. "Can't wait to hear all about it. After we eat. I'm starving."

"Did Max go down for her nap?" I said.

"She's out like a light," Josie said. "I wouldn't be surprised if she sleeps through the night. She's snoring up a storm." Josie glanced at Gerald. "She gets that from her mother."

"Funny," I said, punching her on the shoulder. Then I spotted my mother waving to everyone that dinner was ready. I gave her a golf clap and led the way to our table. “Hey, Gerald. You mind sitting at the other end of the table?”

“What?” the Premier said, walking next to me.

“You know, just in case.”

“You’re a real hoot, Suzy,” he said. “I still can’t believe you put all that together.”

“Oh, we’ve got a long way to go.”

Chapter 5

The rest of us at the table stared as Josie polished off the last of her dinner. She sighed contentedly and wiped her mouth. After a sip of wine, it dawned on her that she was the sole focus of several sets of eyes. Josie sat back in her chair and glanced around the table with a quizzical look on her face.

"What is it? Did I spill something?" she said, giving herself a quick once-over.

"If you did, I'm sure you caught it in your mouth before it landed," Chef Claire deadpanned.

"Yeah," I said, laughing along with everyone else at the table. "Did Captain teach you how to do that mid-air snatch?"

"You guys are a real hoot," Josie said, swirling the wine in her glass before taking another sip. "I notice everyone one at the table is playing with a full belly."

"Well, I for one am impressed," Samantha said. "I thought I could eat. How the heck do you do that?"

"It's a gift," Josie said with a shrug.

"Just ignore them, dear," my mother said. "But I need to thank you."

"For what?"

"You've given me a great idea," my mother said, flashing me a conspiratorial wink.

"This oughta be good," I whispered to Chef Claire.

"Yeah, I smell a setup," Chef Claire said with a grin.

"As you know," my mother said, sitting back in her chair and draping a leg over her knee. "I'm always on the lookout for new summer events we could hold to draw more tourists."

"And?" Josie said, immediately suspicious.

"And what Clay Bay needs, perhaps over the fourth of July weekend, is a good old-fashioned eating contest."

"That's a great idea, Mom," I said, playing along. "Competitive eating events are all the rage."

"Thank you, darling," my mother said with a grin.

"What sort of food would we use?" Chef Claire said. "Maybe hot dogs?"

"Hot dogs would work," my mother said. "Or perhaps we could go with corn on the cob."

"Interesting," I said. "Of course, we couldn't let Josie enter."

"No, of course not," my mother deadpanned. "It wouldn't be fair to the other competitors."

Josie waited out another round of laughter before fixing her stare on my mother.

"I thought you were my friend, Mrs. C."

My mother raised her glass in salute and took a long sip. She spotted me getting to my feet and set her glass down.

"Where are you off to, darling?"

"I'm going to check on Max and then let the dogs out," I said.

"Would you like me to do it?" she said.

"No, you relax, Mom," I said, then glanced back and forth at Josie and Chef Claire. "You guys mind circulating and reminding people not to give the dogs anything to eat. Especially any of the chocolate torte."

"No problem," Chef Claire said, then looked at Josie. "Are you going to be able to walk?"

"Yeah, I think I'll manage," Josie said, making a face at her.

"What kind of dogs do you have?" Samantha said.

"We have four house dogs," I said. "I have an Aussie Shepherd, Josie has a Newfie, and Chef Claire has two of the most gorgeous Goldens you've ever seen."

"Oh, big dogs," Samantha said. "That's great."

"Don't forget Ruby," Chef Claire said.

"That's right," I said. "We have a house guest tonight. Actually, we found her on the beach right after we discovered the body this morning."

"Turns out she was the victim's dog," Chef Claire said.

"Really?" Samantha said. "What kind of dog?"

"Weimaraner," Chef Claire said. "Wait until you see her. She's beautiful."

"What's going to happen to her?" Samantha said.

"That's a good question," I said. "If nobody from the victim's family turns up to claim her, we'll take her to our shelter."

"She'll last about an hour before somebody adopts her," Josie said. "She's a great dog."

"Nobody will be showing up to claim the dog," Samantha said.

"How do you know that?" I said, cocking my head at her.

"Detective Renfro called this afternoon and confirmed the victim didn't have any living family members."

"How did he find that out so fast?" I said, sitting back down at the table.

"He spoke to someone from the FBI," Samantha said. "Apparently, it's something he always does whenever anyone dies under unusual circumstances."

"I guess a suicide victim washing up on a beach meets the definition of unusual," Chef Claire said.

"Yeah, suicide," I said softly as I glanced back and forth at Gerald and Paulie. Then I focused on Samantha. "What did the FBI have to say?"

"Apparently, Quiver was on their radar," she said.

"For what?" I said, rubbing my forehead.

"Detective Renfro didn't go into the details," Samantha said with a shrug. "But the FBI did confirm he didn't have any known family."

I made a mental note to give my friend, Agent Tompkins, a call in the morning and got to my feet. I went inside and found Max sacked out in a deep sleep then headed back outside with the dogs leading the way. All five headed straight for our table to say hello. Ruby took an immediate liking to Samantha and placed her front paws on her shoulders and licked her face.

"Look at her," Samantha gushed as she stroked the dog's head.

"Somebody likes you," Josie said with a laugh.

"What did you say her name was?" Samantha said, hugging the dog whose tail was working overtime.

"Ruby," Josie said.

"Oh, my goodness," Samantha said. "She's exactly the kind of dog I've been looking for. Would it be possible for me to adopt her?"

Josie and I glanced at each other then shrugged in tandem.

"I don't see why not," Josie said.

"Sure, she's obviously going to a good home," I said, making room for Chloe on my lap. I grunted when she landed. "You're getting too big for this."

"Good luck convincing her of that," Josie said, giving Captain's side a gentle thump.

"Thank you so much," Samantha said, hugging the Weimaraner again before glancing back and forth at the house dogs. "And who are these guys?"

"This is Captain," Josie said. "The big fur ball in Suzy's lap is Chloe. And those two are Al and Dente."

"Al dente?" Samantha said, then chuckled. "That's funny. Great names for a chef's dogs."

"There they are," my mother said when she spotted a woman and two young teenage girls strolling across the lawn.

All four house dogs spotted the familiar guests and made a beeline for them. The Weimaraner, not wanting to be left out, sprinted after them. Soon, the two girls were rolling around on the grass with the dogs. Teresa approached the table and shared hugs with all of us.

"You made it," I said.

"Sorry we're late," Teresa said. "We were on our way when I got a call about a stray on the side of the road."

"Is the dog okay?" Josie said, sitting up in her chair.

"I think she's fine," Teresa said. "But she's favoring her front left leg. I know you're not working tomorrow, but would you mind swinging by the shelter in the morning?"

"No problem," Josie said. "What kind of dog?"

"She looks like a Maltese mix of some sort," Teresa said, then glanced back at her daughters who were still playing with the dogs. "Beautiful Weimaraner. Where did she come from?"

"We found her on the beach this morning," I said. "Where's Rocco?"

"He's on a call with the restaurant," Teresa said.

"Is there a problem?" Chef Claire said.

"No, he's dealing with tomorrow's order. He'll be here soon. Is there any food left? I'm starving."

"Tons," I said, then spotted Samantha. "I don't think you know Samantha. She's down here relieving Jimmy while he's on vacation."

"Nice to meet you," Teresa said.

"You too," Samantha said.

"Teresa runs the local shelter I was telling you about," I said. "Hi, girls. How are you doing?"

"Hi, Suzy," the older of Teresa's daughters said. "Mom, did you see the Weimaraner? She'd be perfect."

"Here we go," Teresa said with a laugh. "These two have been driving me nuts about getting another dog."

"A big dog," the younger daughter said, correcting her mother.

"We'll talk about it later," Teresa said. "But you guys need to eat first."

"Let's go take a look and see what we have on the grill," my mother said, getting to her feet.

She and the two girls headed off, and Teresa sat down and began chatting with Josie. I spotted Gerald sitting by himself at the other end of the table. I sat down next to him and couldn't miss the look of concern on his face.

"You look like a man with a lot on his mind," I said with a grin.

"I always have a lot on my mind," he said, not returning the smile.

"I'd really like to see that letter."

"Swing by my office in the morning," he said.

"Yeah. Your office," I said with a frown.

"I'm sure everyone has forgotten all about those incidents," he said, finally breaking into a smile.

"Oh, I seriously doubt that," I said.

Both of my two prior visits to Gerald's office, through no fault of our own, had ended up with his executive assistant entering and finding us in what appeared to be compromising positions. The first visit I was dealing with severe sunburn and wearing a pair of baggy shorts that had fallen down when I tripped and fell on the floor. The second time I choked on a piece of hard candy. Gerald had been behind me applying the Heimlich maneuver when his assistant walked in. The two incidents had earned me the reputation around his office as one of the Premier's *special friends*, and his assistant continued to take great delight in tormenting both of us.

"Just stay on the other side of the desk and we'll be fine," Gerald deadpanned.

"Yeah, I'll do my best," I said, making a face at him. "You're worried about this, aren't you?"

"A bit," he said. "And I don't like the idea that the FBI is involved."

"If you haven't done anything, there's nothing to worry about, right?"

"It's the FBI," he said. "There's always something to worry about when they're around."

"Sure, I get that," I said, nodding. Then a question bubbled up to the surface. "Do you mind if I ask you something?"

"Would it matter if I did?"

"Probably not."

"That's what I thought. What do you want to know?"

"Where's the fifty million you had frozen?"

He sat quietly as he stared off into the distance.

"It must be around somewhere," he said eventually.

I laughed.

"Gerald, it must be around somewhere is something you'd say when you're wondering where your phone is. We're talking about fifty million bucks."

"Actually, we're not talking about that," he said, making solid eye contact.

"Did you take the money?"

"What part of we're not talking about it didn't you understand, Suzy?"

"Okay," I said. "We'll stick a pin in that one for now," I said. "We'll circle back later."

Gerald exhaled audibly and shook his head. Then he slapped his thighs and got to his feet.

"I think I'll go grab a slice of that torte before Josie eats it all," he said.

"Good call," I said, deep in thought. "I'll see you in the morning."

"I'm sure it will be the highlight of my day," he said.

"Funny," I said, then watched him stroll off in search of something delicious to take his mind off his problems.

Chapter 6

After the daily torture of my morning run, I showered then dropped Max off with my mother and Paulie at her place next door. On the drive to Gerald's office, a visit I was not looking forward to, I placed a call to Agent Tompkins at the FBI. He answered on the second ring.

"Suzy Chandler," he said warmly. "How the hell are you?"

"I'm great. And you?"

"Busy, but good. Keeping the country safe is a fulltime job."

"Yeah, I've heard the rumor," I said, laughing.

"Are you guys spending the winter at your place on Cayman?"

"Yeah. And it's been sweltering the past couple of weeks."

"Poor baby. It's fifteen and snowing here."

"Yuk. Do you have time to talk?"

"Sure, I've got a few minutes. What do you need?"

"I was wondering if you could answer a few questions about a guy named William Quiver?"

"Quiver?" he said. "The name rings a bell, but nothing comes to mind. Who is he?"

"His father was Slash Quiver," I said.

"Holy crap," Agent Tompkins said. "Slash Quiver. I haven't thought about him since he died. What's his kid up to?"

"I was hoping you could tell me," I said, pulling off the side of the road to concentrate.

"Give me a sec while I check the system and see if there's anything I can share with you."

I listened to the clack of his keyboard, then it went quiet for several moments.

"Okay," he said. "I can confirm we have an open file on William Quiver, aka Little Billy."

"Why are you looking at him?" I said.

"Not so fast, Suzy. Why are you asking?"

"Because Chef Claire and I found his body on the beach yesterday during our morning run."

"I don't know what's more shocking," Agent Tompkins said with a laugh. "The fact the guy is dead, or that you've started jogging."

"Everybody's a comedian."

"How did he die?"

"That's where it gets interesting," I said. "The cops found a suicide note in his pocket, but Paulie knew the guy and is convinced there's no way Little Billy would have done that."

"Paulie? That's your mom's boyfriend, right?"

"That's him."

"He's the one who used to be some sort of criminal," Agent Tompkins said.

"Ancient history," I said. "But Paulie did work on the dark side for a while. And he had history with Slash and knew Little Billy."

"Okay," he said. "Color me intrigued."

"Is there anything in his file about his religious background?" I said.

"Hang on. Let me take a look…Yeah, there's a note about some ancient branch of Christianity the family belonged to. Why do you want to know?"

"That's the reason Paulie has for why the guy wouldn't have committed suicide," I said.

"Sounds a little thin," Agent Tompkins said. "But I suppose it's possible. You say he's convinced somebody killed the guy?"

"He's positive."

"So, whoever did it is trying to make it look like a suicide. Right down to leaving a note."

"That's what it looks like," I said.

"Was the note in Little Billy's handwriting?"

"I'm not sure," I said, chastising myself for not asking the question. I made a mental note to check with Detective Renfro then continued. "Do you have a local address for the guy?"

"We do," Agent Tompkins said.

"Can I have it?"

"No, you may not."

"C'mon, Agent Tompkins. What harm can it do?"

"Given our prior history, Suzy, I can think of several possibilities."

"It's not like I'm gonna just drive over there and check the place out," I said, protesting.

"Then I guess there's no reason why you need the address, right?" he said, laughing.

"Why are you being so difficult?"

"Well, it's kinda my job. Ask the local cops for the address."

"Fine," I said, pouting. "What was Little Billy doing that got your attention?"

"You're like a pit bull," he said. "Let's say he was involved in something he shouldn't have been doing?"

"Dealing drugs?"

"Nope."

"Laundering money?"

"Nope."

"What was it then?"

"Nope."

"You're stuck on repeat, Agent Tompkins."

"Nice to see you're paying attention. Just let it go, Suzy. Whoever decided to kill him, if in fact he was murdered, probably did the planet a favor."

"Fine. I was going to invite you down here to spend a week with us but never mind," I said.

"Thanks for the offer, but I couldn't possibly get away at the moment."

"Why are you being so difficult?"

"Because it's none of your business, Suzy."

"Just one more question."

"Nope."

"Really? I can't ask you one more?"

"Oh, sure, you can ask. I was just practicing my response."

I bit my bottom lip to stem the flow of an extended string of expletives that was on the tip of my tongue then took a few deep breaths.

"Can you tell me anything about Quiver's bank accounts?"

"Bank accounts?" Agent Tompkins said. "I doubt it, but what do you want to know?"

"The old man, Slash, apparently had an account down here," I said.

"A big-time heroin dealer? I'd be shocked if he hadn't."

"I heard the account got frozen," I said.

"Where did you hear that?" Agent Tompkins said.

"I have my sources."

The FBI agent fell silent and I waited it out.

"Oh, that's right," he said eventually. "You're buddies with the Premier down there. How is Gerald?"

"Do you know Gerald?" I said, surprised.

"Only by reputation."

"What sort of reputation are you talking about?"

"Suzy, the guy heads the government of one of the biggest money-laundering wonderlands on the planet. You really think we wouldn't be keeping a close eye on all the major players down there?"

"I guess I never thought about it," I said. "But I suppose it makes sense."

"So, Gerald told you about the frozen account?"

"Nope."

"Okay, I guess I deserved that," he said with a chuckle. "What do you want to know?"

"How much money is in the account?"

"Right now?"

"Yeah."

"Hang on," he said, then began tapping his keyboard. "I guess I can share one tidbit with you."

"Oh, goodie," I said, paying close attention.

"Since his old man's demise and our initial look into his affairs, I can tell you the account balance hasn't changed to this day."

"That's a relief," I said, crossing one of the questions I had for Gerald off my list.

"Why is that a relief?" Agent Tompkins said, turning suspicious.

"Oh, it's nothing. It's just I'm glad to hear nobody has been messing around with the account."

"Suzy, it's my turn to ask you a question."

"Go ahead."

"How deep have you got yourself into this thing?"

"Not deep at all," I said, then forced a laugh. "Yet."

"That's what I was afraid of," he said.

"I'll be fine, Agent Tompkins. So, the balance hasn't changed since the old man died?"

"No, it hasn't. It's been showing a balance of one dollar for close to twenty years."

"I'm sorry. Did you say a dollar?"

"Yeah, one American greenback. You sound surprised. How much were you expecting to be in it?"

"Fifty," I whispered.

"Fifty thousand?"

"Nope."

"Million?"

"Yeah," I grunted into the phone.

"Wow," he said. "What do you know? Fifty million has gone missing."

"I'm sure it's around somewhere."

"I'm glad you called, Suzy," Agent Tompkins said.

"You change your mind about telling me what Little Billy did that put him on your radar?"

He laughed loudly into the phone.

"Yeah, I suppose it's the least I can do. But if you're going to dig into this one, you have to promise to keep the local cops in the loop."

"Sure, sure,"' I said, nodding to myself.

"I'm serious, Suzy. Keep the freelancing to a minimum. There's a reason why that place is so attractive to folks trying to keep people like me from looking too closely into what they're doing with their money. And they're not shy about biting back when people start snooping around."

"Yeah, I get it. So, what was Little Billy up to?"

"All I can say is he liked to dabble in technology," Agent Tompkins said.

"Technology?" I said, frowning as I let my mind ponder the possibilities. "Well, I doubt if he was building websites or working in a call center." I fell silent and encouraged my neurons to fire. A possibility drifted to the surface, and I gave it some serious consideration before continuing. "Huh," I grunted after a lengthy silence. "He was a hacker, wasn't he?"

"Son of a gun," Agent Tompkins whispered.

"I'm right, aren't I? He was some sort of financial hacker. And where better to do it than in a place where money laundering is encouraged."

"Encouraged is too strong of a word," Agent Tompkins said, correcting me. "They've tightened things up a lot over the past several years."

"How about tolerated?"

"Yeah, that's probably more accurate," he said.

"Little Billy was hacking the accounts of people who'd made their money from illegal activities. And that makes it hard for them to report the money as stolen, right?"

"A lot of times, yes," he said.

"Hacking into criminals' bank accounts and stealing their ill-gotten gains," I said, nodding. "That's brilliant. But somebody must have figured out what he was doing."

"Unbelievable," Agent Tompkins said softly. "You sure you don't want to come work for me?"

"Would I be able to bring the dogs to work?" I said, chuckling.

"No."

"Then I'll pass," I said, rubbing my forehead. "Are you going to do some digging of your own?"

"Oh, you can count on it. But I don't like our chances. Twenty years is a long time. And I doubt if there's any trail about where that fifty million went."

"Yeah, maybe on your end."

"What?"

"Nothing," I said, anxious to end the call and get to Gerald's office. "I need to run."

"Okay. It was nice chatting with you, Suzy. But promise me you'll keep your eyes open and your head down."

"Will do. Have a nice day, Agent Tompkins."

"You too. And say hi to Chef Claire for me."

"You got it. And if you do have a chance to get down here, you're more than welcome to stay with us."

"I don't like my chances," Agent Tompkins said. "Stay safe."

I ended the call and put the previously removed question back on the list. Twenty years was a long time. But fifty million was a lot of money.

Chapter 7

I glanced around the foyer while I waited for security to confirm my appointment with Gerald then took the elevator up. As I strolled down the hall, I waved to a few people I recognized and did my best to ignore the look one of Gerald's staff gave me. I couldn't help but wonder how much my two previous encounters had been embellished through the office grapevine, and I had a pretty clear idea they might live in infamy and be passed down to the next generation of workers. As I approached the large desk sitting outside the Premier's office, I took a few deep breaths and prepared myself for what was coming.

"Good morning, Marjorie," I said, smiling at the stylish, older woman sitting behind the desk.

"Hello, Suzy," Gerald's executive assistant said, beaming at me. "It's been too long."

"Ya think?" I said with a frown. "We must have a different opinion on that subject."

"Oh, that," she said, waving it off. "We've all forgotten about those incidents. It could have happened to anyone."

"Unfortunately, it happened to me," I said.

"Yes, it did, didn't it?" she said with an evil grin. "Let me check and see if he's ready for you." She made the call and waited. "Suzy Chandler is here, sir…Of course, I'll send her right in." She gently placed the receiver back in its cradle and gestured at the closed door. "He's all yours."

"Thanks, Marjorie," I said, surprised by her lack of comment.

"Enjoy your meeting," she said, then called after me. "Oh, should I order champagne or will this just be a *quickie*?"

"You're a real hoot, Marjorie," I said, glancing back at her before opening the door.

Her laughter followed me into the office, and I spotted Gerald getting up out of his chair. He grabbed an envelope off the desk and motioned for me to take a seat on the couch. I sat down and glanced around the enormous office as I waited for him to get settled in the chair directly across from me.

"Did she give you a hard time?" Gerald said, nodding at the door.

"She asked if we wanted champagne or if this was going to be a quickie," I said with a scowl.

"Don't worry about it. It keeps her young. Thanks again for the party last night. I had a great time."

"It didn't look like it," I said, studying his face.

"I was just tired," he said, waving it off. Then he handed me the envelope. "It's a short letter. But straight to the point."

I read the brief message twice, then handed it back to him. He slid the letter back into the envelope then tossed it on the coffee table. I sat back on the couch with a deep frown on my face.

"What is it?" Gerald said.

"I was expecting some sort of blackmail request."

"I wondered about that myself. But I imagine Little Billy was saving it for when we met," Gerald said, reaching for the bowl of hard candy sitting on the coffee table. He held it out but I shook my head.

"Thanks, but I'll pass."

"What are the odds that could happen again?" he said, laughing.

"Probably a million to one," I said, grabbing a small handful of bite-sized from my bag. "But these will do just fine." I popped one of the chocolate morsels as I pondered the message. "The sins of my father are no excuse for your actions. Well, you're right. He definitely got straight to the point."

"Yes, he did."

"Did he call you or follow up after you got the letter?"

"No. And when I heard he committed suicide, I thought I'd caught an enormous break."

"I imagine you did."

"You're convinced he was murdered?" Gerald said, leaning forward.

"I am," I said, rubbing my forehead. "And I'm starting to have my doubts it was Little Billy who sent that letter."

"Why would somebody do that?"

"To give you a motive for killing him," I said.

"But why would they bother to stage his suicide?"

"That seems to be the fifty-million-dollar question on the table, doesn't it?" I said, raising an eyebrow at him.

"Don't start, Suzy," he said, his voice rising. Then he forced himself to calm down by taking a few deep breaths. "Who do you think could have sent the letter?"

"I suppose it could have been one of the people Little Billy hacked," I said with a shrug.

"I think I'm going to need a bit more," Gerald said, sitting back and draping a leg over his knee.

"Apparently, he was a well-known hacker who liked to go into criminals' bank accounts and empty them out. Especially accounts located in offshore financial havens."

"You're joking, right?"

"No."

"I know I'm going to hate the answer, but I need to ask. How on earth do you know that?"

"I talked with a friend at the FBI on my way over here," I said softly.

"You did what?" Gerald said, both eyebrows going way up.

"I wanted to find out if Little Billy had been on the FBI's radar," I whispered.

"Geez, Suzy, I've got enough to worry about running the government," he said, shaking his head. "And your friend at the Bureau told you what he was up to?"

"Well, I kinda put two and two together," I said, shrugging again.

"Of course. Why am I not surprised?" he said, then his expression morphed into concern. "Did my name come up during your conversation?"

"Maybe," I said, forcing a small smile.

"Ah, crap," Gerald snapped. "What did you talk about?"

"Nothing, really. He happened to mention he was familiar with you. And that the Feebs keep a close eye on things down here."

"Is that all?"

"Yeah, pretty much," I said, after replaying the conversation in my head.

"Okay, I can live with that."

"How many FBI agents are walking around down here?"

"I have no idea," Gerald said. "I know most of the official ones, but I'm sure the Bureau has several undercover agents on the island."

"Well, you do run billions of dollars through your banking system," I said. "Follow the money, right?"

"What else did you and your friend talk about?"

I sat back and fell silent as I formulated the best way to have the conversation that was top of mind for me. I popped another bite-sized to stall for time, then swallowed and stared at the Premier.

"We talked about Slash's bank account," I whispered.

He flinched like I'd slapped him and stared at me in disbelief.

"And?" Gerald said, leaning forward in his chair.

"And he told me the balance in the account hasn't changed since the old man died," I said. "It's still one dollar."

"Son of a bitch," Gerald said in a violent whisper.

"That's one way to put it," I said, continuing to study him. "Where's the fifty million, Gerald?"

"It's around somewhere," he said, a small smile emerging. "Actually, it's quite close."

"Don't tell me you keep it here in your office?" I said, making a face at him.

"No, of course not," he said, getting to his feet. "Follow me."

"Why? You got a trap door in the floor I don't know about?"

"I wish," he said, heading for the far side of the office. "C'mon. I need to show you something."

I followed him to the large picture window that offered an expansive view of George Town. I glanced out the window then looked over at him.

"What am I looking at?"

"Over there," he said, pointing.

"All I see is the hospital."

"Fifty beds. Including a state-of-the-art Emergency Room, the Women and Children's Health Center, Wellness Center, and a dental clinic."

"That's where the money went?"

Yes," Gerald said, nodding as he beamed at me.

"You gave them the money to build that?"

"I did. Actually, we both did."

"You mean the banker who helped you get your hands on Slash's money, right?"

"Yes, Robert was the bank president," Gerald said. "It was his idea to leave a dollar in the account so it didn't show up on any reports as closed."

"Is he still around?" I said.

"No, right after that, he retired and left the island. I have no idea where he ended up."

Knowing what I did about Gerald's personality, especially the size of his ego, which I was certain was a prerequisite for a career in politics, the inevitable question bubbled to the surface.

"If you gave them the money to build the hospital, why isn't your name on it?"

"I wanted it to be anonymous," he said, avoiding eye contact.

"Sorry, Gerald, I'm not buying it. A politician not wanting to take credit for something nice they've done is like Michelangelo telling admirers of the Sistine Chapel; 'Oh, that. It was nothing.'"

"I wasn't in politics at that time."

"No, but you were certainly thinking about getting into the game."

"When did you get so cynical?" Gerald said, turning toward me.

"You couldn't put your name on it because you didn't want people asking questions about where you got the money, right?" I said.

"Yeah, that's as good an explanation as any," he said nodding.

I glanced back out the window, then another thought bubbled to the surface.

"Hang on."

"What is it now?" he said.

"If you had told people you were the one who donated fifty million of confiscated drug money to fund a local hospital, you would have been a hero. Your story would have been that you investigated criminal activity, put a stop to it, and then used the money to create something special for the folks who live here. And it would have been the perfect way to jumpstart your political career."

"I never really gave it much thought," he whispered.

"Horse pucky. I'm willing to bet it was all you thought about for weeks before you handed the money over." I studied his expression before continuing. "How much did it cost to build the hospital?"

"Almost fifty million," he said.

I nodded and looked back out the window at the impressive structure I had driven by dozens of times. Then my neurons surged, and I stared at him in disbelief.

"Hang on."

"Now what?"

"*Almost*?"

Gerald gnawed on his bottom lip then shrugged.

"We may have kept a little for ourselves," he said eventually.

"How much?"

"Is that really any of your business, Suzy?"

"No, but it's never stopped me before. How much did you keep?"

"Two million," he said. "But I had to split it with Robert."

"You once told me you bought your house about twenty years ago for a million bucks," I said. "That was the money you used to buy it, right?"

"Yeah."

"Geez, Gerald," I said, starting to pace back and forth in front of the window. "Well, now I understand why it had to be anonymous."

"That was certainly a major reason," he said softly as he looked out at the hospital.

"But not the only one, right?"

"No."

"You couldn't go public because you were worried about what the people you stole it from would do to you."

Gerald flinched when he heard my reference to stealing and turned defensive.

"I have no regrets about building that hospital, regardless of where the money came from."

"What about the million you kept for yourself?"

"Nobody ever missed it," he said.

"Apparently, Little Billy did."

"Who cares? He and his father were a stain on society."

"You might want to keep that opinion to yourself. You know, in case the cops ever ask you about them."

"That's certainly my working plan at the moment," Gerald said, forcing a tight-lipped smile.

"Who else knows about this?"

"Only a few people I trust completely."

I nodded, briefly glanced back out at the hospital, then cocked my head at him.

"My mother."

"What about her?"

"Does she know what you did?"

"Of course. I trust your mother with my life," he said with a shrug. "And it was her idea to build the Women and Children's facility. She even kicked in a million bucks of her own money."

"She's never said a word," I said, frowning.

"That's the anonymous part," Gerald said, then laughed. "And maybe she was worried about your ability to keep your mouth shut."

"Hey, I'm great with secrets," I said, my voice rising. "To this day, nobody knows a thing about Josie's escapades down in Mexico during spring break. Or her short stint in jail."

"Josie was in jail?" Gerald said, stunned by the news.

I gnawed on my bottom lip as I chastised myself for letting that little tidbit slip.

"Oops," I whispered. "Forget I said that."

"I'll make you a deal," he said, flashing me his trademark smile. "Are you going to tell anybody about this?"

"No," I said, shaking my head. "It'll be our little secret, Gerald."

"Then Josie's secret is safe with me," he said, pulling me in close for a long hug. "Thanks, Suzy."

"Some things should remain secret," I said, squeezing back.

"What sort of things should be kept secret?"

We both flinched and broke our embrace when we heard the voice. Marjorie's head was poking through the open door. I didn't need a map to decipher the look on her face.

"I'm sorry. I knocked but nobody answered," she said, chagrined. "It looks like I walked in on something."

"Don't worry, Marjorie," I said, recovering. "I was just telling Gerald it's probably best if our torrid affair remains a secret."

"Right," Gerald said, clearing his throat. "Our affair. Thanks for stopping by, Suzy."

"I just wanted to let you know your eleven o'clock has arrived," Marjorie said, then shook her head and closed the door.

"Smooth," Gerald said, laughing.

"Yeah, but don't get any ideas," I said, gently punching him on the shoulder.

"Hey, you could do a lot worse," he said in mock protest.

"Yeah, but I don't think I could handle conjugal visits while you were in prison," I deadpanned.

"Don't even joke about that."

"Then stop taking money that doesn't belong to you," I said.

"I was young and ambitious," he said, leading me to the door.

"What's your excuse these days?"

"Cheap shot," he said, giving me a playful shove toward the exit. "Goodbye, Suzy. See you at the restaurant tonight?"

"You will. Just promise to keep your hands to yourself," I said, grinning at him.

"I'll do my best," he said. "But I have to say you look great. Chef Claire has whipped you into shape."

"She's a tyrant. But don't tell her I said that. She'll make me run an extra mile."

Chapter 8

I gently grabbed Max's hand who was smiling and gurgling at me from the comfort of her car seat. My mother glanced through the rear-view mirror and beamed when she spotted us.

"She loves riding in the car," my mother said.

"She does," I said. "I should have had her years ago."

"Why's that, darling?"

"Because it's the first thing that's ever stopped you from driving a hundred miles an hour everywhere you go," I said, laughing. "We could have walked to the restaurant faster than this."

"Yeah," Josie said from the passenger seat. "Pick up the pace, Mrs. C. Some of us need sustenance."

"I'm sure you'll survive it, dear," my mother deadpanned as she focused on the road in front of us then flipped the turn signal on and slowed down even more. "Safety first."

"We've still got a mile to go to the restaurant," Josie said. "Why do you have your turn signal on?"

"I'm just letting people know my intentions," my mother said, her hands gripping the steering wheel at ten and two.

I glanced over at Paulie who was sitting on the other side of the car seat, and he merely shrugged my mother's behavior off.

"What's your secret?" I whispered to him as I nodded at my mother.

"Rule number one. Don't worry about what you can't control," he whispered back.

"Hey, that's pretty good advice," I said, laughing. "Hey, Josie. I forgot to ask. Did Samantha stop by to pick up the Weimaraner?"

"She did," Josie said, turning halfway around in her seat. "I feel good about pairing those two up."

"Yeah, the dog seemed to have an instant bond with her," I said, then glanced down at Max who continued to stare at me. "Didn't she, Max?"

Max kicked her legs and held her arms out for me to pick her up.

"Hang on," I said softly. "We'll get there…eventually."

"Funny, darling," my mother said, her eyes rotating between the road in front and all three mirrors.

Mercifully, a few minutes later, my mother parked in her reserved spot in front of the restaurant. I unbuckled the car seat and gently lifted Max out and set her on my lap. Josie opened the back door, and I handed the baby to her before climbing out of the SUV. Josie passed the baby back, and we headed up the steps and entered the crowded restaurant. Rocco greeted us at the door and traced a finger along Max's cheek before glancing around.

"Good evening. You guys having a drink at the bar or do you want to head straight to your table?" he said.

"Table," Josie said, pointing in the direction of the dining room.

"Yeah, that's probably a good idea," I said to my mother. "Let's get some food in her. I really don't want to deal with her whining about how hungry she is."

"Good call, darling."

"She doesn't look hungry," Rocco cooed, again stroking Max's cheek. "And you're not a whiner, are you?"

"I think they were referring to me," Josie said, glaring at my mother and me.

"Oh, then that's definitely a good call," Rocco said, laughing as he waved us into the dining room. "Follow me."

We sat down at the table, and after I made sure Max was secured in her high chair, I grabbed a bottle of milk from my bag. She held it with both hands and began sucking contentedly as she glanced around the restaurant.

"She's such a good girl," my mother gushed before picking up her menu.

"What are you having?" I said to Josie, who hadn't even bothered to open the menu.

"New York. Au gratin potatoes, spinach," she said, reaching for the bread basket.

"Sounds great," I said. "Paulie?"

"I can't resist the crab curry," he said, taking a slice of bread from the basket Josie was holding out.

"No, thank you," my mother said, waving the bread away. "Crab curry it is." She closed her menu then focused on me. "How was your meeting with Gerald?"

"It was…interesting," I said, dredging a piece of bread through olive oil. "And quite informative."

"Do tell," Josie said.

"No, I don't think I should say anything," I said, shaking my head.

"Ooh, I smell dirt," Josie said with a grin.

"Come on, darling. I'm sure he didn't tell you anything the rest of us don't already know."

"No, I better not," I said, then took a big bite of bread to stall for time, hoping they'd lose interest in the topic.

"Spill," Josie said.

"Well, I can tell you one thing," I said. "Gerald's executive assistant thinks he and I are having a torrid affair."

"Why on earth would she think that?" my mother said.

"Because I kinda told her we were," I said with a shrug.

"Oh, my God," my mother said, sitting upright in her chair. "You're not, are you?"

"Of course not," I snapped. "He's too-"

"Old?" Josie said.

"No," I said, scowling at her.

"Too much of a player?" Josie said, turning relentless.

"Stop," I said.

"Too busy? You know, he can't spend enough *quality* time with you?"

"Shouldn't you be stuffing your face?" I said, pushing the bread basket toward her.

"At the moment, this sounds even better," Josie said, then glanced around the table. "And that's saying a lot. You know how much I love this bread."

"Yeah, I could probably ballpark it," I said, then noticed Max's bottle starting to slip out of her hands. I held it until she regained her grip, then reached for my water.

"Well, if you felt the need to tell such a whopper to Marjorie, then whatever you're trying to keep quiet must be huge," my mother said, giving me her best stare as she placed both elbows on the table.

I felt all six eyes boring into my head, and I finally nodded.

"Okay, I guess a little bit couldn't hurt," I said, leaning forward.

"I knew she'd fold," Josie said, laughing.

"Like clockwork," my mother, laughing along.

I turned defensive as I glared at my mother.

"Fine," I said. "We talked about the hospital. Why didn't you ever tell me you donated a million bucks to help build the Women and Children's wing?"

"Wow," my mother said, stunned. "You did have quite the conversation, didn't you?"

"We did," I said. "And you've also never told me about Gerald's anonymous gift of the money to build it."

"No, I most certainly did not," she said. "And please keep your voice down, darling."

I leaned in closer.

"Why didn't you tell me?"

"Because some things should remain a secret," my mother said softly. "And to be honest, I didn't think you'd be able to keep it to yourself."

"Gerald donated money to build a hospital?" Paulie said with a frown.

"He donated a lot of money," I said, glancing over at him.

"How much?"

"Almost fifty million," I whispered.

Paulie choked on a sip of water and barely avoided spitting it across the table.

"You see, darling," my mother said. "That's exactly why I didn't tell you."

"Fifty million?" Paulie said, still stunned by the news. "Where on earth did he get his hands on fifty million dollars?"

"It doesn't matter," my mother said, then glared at me. "What is wrong with you?"

"Me? You were the one who insisted I tell you what we talked about," I said, returning her stare.

"You simply can't be trusted with sensitive information," she said.

"I most certainly can," I said, for some reason momentarily turning back into a teenager.

My mother snorted and waved my comment off.

"I never told you about the time Josie was in a Mexican jail, did I?" I blurted, then flinched when she kicked me under the table. "Ow, knock it off."

"Then shut it," Josie said.

"Oh, I gotta hear this one," Paulie said, grinning at Josie.

"Not gonna happen," Josie snapped, then gave me a long, deep scowl.

"Please, dear," my mother said to Josie. "You simply must give us some of the details."

"It was spring break," Josie said, reaching for another piece of bread. "Use your imagination."

"Oh, I'm way ahead of you," Paulie said, laughing.

"Funny," Josie said, drowning her bread in olive oil. Then she glared at me again. "I hope you're happy. I told you that in confidence."

"Lesson learned," my mother said. "Darling, I have to ask. Gerald never talks about that situation. Why on earth did he feel the need to mention it to you?"

Cornered like a rat, I gave Max a thorough once-over to buy some time. I glanced at my mother and knew instinctively she wouldn't be letting it go. Eventually, I nodded at her.

"I might have asked him about it," I whispered.

"Okay. That raises a few interesting questions. One in particular. How on earth did you find out about the money?"

"Well, he mentioned the fifty million last night at the party. He was telling me about the letter he received the other day. Gerald was pretty sure it came from Little Billy Quiver, and when he heard he'd committed suicide, he thought he'd caught a huge break. Then when I told him Paulie's theory about why Quiver wouldn't have killed himself, we started talking about how Gerald had frozen the old man's account."

"Okay," my mother said, nodding. "But that doesn't explain how you found out about what happened to the money."

"No, it doesn't," I said, avoiding eye contact as I fiddled with my cutlery.

"Hang on," Josie said, confused. "If Gerald managed to put a stop to some criminal activity, then donated all the money to build a hospital, why wouldn't he be shouting that from a rooftop?"

I looked at my mother, and she eventually shrugged then nodded for me to continue.

"Because he kept some of it for himself," I whispered.

"Oh, crap," Josie said, shaking her head. "What on earth was he thinking?"

"That there was a certain house he just had to get his hands on," my mother said, refilling her wine glass.

"Well, it's a great house," I said with a shrug. "Let's hope he's able to keep living there."

"Exactly," my mother said. "And that's why this is going to be the last time we discuss this."

"We're talking about a murder case, Mom. A murder Gerald is being set up for."

"I'm very aware of that, darling," she snapped. "But it has nothing to do with that hospital or where the money came from to build it."

"I'm gonna have to disagree with you," I said, then flinched when I caught the look on her face. "But you're right, there's probably no reason it needs to get out."

"Thank you," she said as she settled back into her chair for a moment before placing her elbows back on the table and giving me another laser-like stare. "Hang on. You still haven't answered my question about how you found out the money was missing from the account."

I felt my face begin to redden, and I took a small sip of wine before responding.

"I called Agent Tompkins this morning."

"You called the FBI?" my mother said, gripping the edge of the table as her eyes grew wide.

"Yes, Mom."

"Why would you do that?"

"I wanted to find out if Little Billy was on the Feebs' radar," I said. "But I was only approaching it from the murder perspective. You know, I wanted to see if I could find anything that might help Gerald get out from under a possible murder charge."

"Then how did the money come up?" my mother said, her intense stare relentless.

"I asked about the account," I said.

"Damn," my mother whispered. "What did Agent Tompkins tell you?"

"Just that there was a dollar in the account that had been there for twenty years," I said, dreading thc weight of the penny that was about to drop.

My mother gave my response some thought as she sipped her wine. Then her eyes flared into an owlish expression. She set her glass down on the table and wiped her mouth.

"Are you telling me the FBI had no idea there used to be fifty million dollars in the account?"

"Yes," I whispered. "I'm so sorry, Mom.

"Damn it," she snapped, then fired her napkin down at the table. She got to her feet and focused on Paulie. "We're leaving."

"But we haven't had dinner yet," Paulie said, confused by her outburst.

"Get it to go," my mother said. "I'll be in the car."

"Mom, wait," I said, starting to get up from my chair.

Josie placed a hand on my arm and shook her head at me.

"Try not to be too long," my mother said to Paulie before giving me a final look of anger and disgust. "Do you have any idea about the potential problems you've created?"

“I’m sorry, Mom,” I said.

But I doubt if she heard me since she was already halfway to the front door. Paulie watched her departure then got to his feet.

“I’ll pick up our orders at the bar,” he said. “Don’t worry, I’ll talk to her.”

“Good luck,” I said between deep breaths. “Don’t let her drive.”

“Not a chance,” Paulie said, then departed with a small wave.

“Wow,” Josie said. “She’s pissed.”

“Yeah. This is a bad one,” I said.

“Has she ever been that mad at you before?”

“A couple of times. But it’s been a long time.”

“Well, you’ll need to fix it, won’t you?”

“How the hell am I gonna do that?”

“The same way you always do,” Josie said. “By figuring out who killed Little Billy Quiver.”

“I suppose you’re right,” I said, nodding.

“And hopefully keeping your mouth shut in the process. I can’t believe you spilled the beans about Mexico.”

“Yeah, sorry about that.”

“I should be mad,” she said.

“Have you forgotten about kicking me under the table?”

“Oh, that,” she said, waving it off. “Involuntary reaction to bad news.”

“I see,” I said, managing a small smile. “So, you’ve forgiven me?”

“Let’s not get ahead of ourselves. But if I did choose to stay mad at you tonight, that would be me just piling on.”

“Like kicking a puppy?”

“Oh, you’re way past puppy, Suzy. And that’s part of the reason your mom reacted the way she did.”

I gave her comment some thought, then nodded and clinked glasses with her. We ate a heavy meal, the table shrouded by intermittent dark clouds of extended silence.

Chapter 9

Max giggled as she reached out to pat Chloe's nose who was sitting in the water next to us on the top step of the pool. Chloe nuzzled her tiny hand then gently licked it, producing a squeal of delight. Max splashed the water with both hands and thrust her legs back and forth. I tightened my grip around her waist and shook my head at Josie and Chef Claire who were stretched out on separate rafts and drifting nearby.

"I almost dropped her," I said. "She's getting so strong."

"Yup," Josie said, not bothering to open her eyes. "Just wait until she starts walking."

"It won't be long," Chef Claire said as she paddled with one hand to the edge of the pool. "You did great this morning."

"Thanks," I said, still preoccupied with the events of last night at the restaurant.

"Define great," Josie said, opening one eye and raising an arm to block the sun.

"She did three miles and barely said a word the entire time," Chef Claire said, then laughed. "Not a whine in sight."

"That is great," Josie deadpanned. "What's your secret?"

"Shut it," I said, splashing her.

"You still preoccupied with your mom?" Josie said, sliding off the raft and sitting down on the steps next to me.

"Yeah. I think I blew it."

"Because you've managed to get the FBI looking into one of her best friends?" she said.

"Yeah, there is that," I said, setting Max on my lap.

"Someone who just happens to run the government down here," Josie said.

"I'll fix it," I said, then stared across the lawn in the direction of my mother's house. "You think she'll still show up?"

"Are you kidding?" Chef Claire said. "And pass up the chance to spend the day with her granddaughter?"

"Nuclear winter wouldn't stop her," Josie said, laughing. Then she nodded at the back gate. "Speaking of grumpy moms, there she is. Right on time."

I watched my mother casually stroll in our direction. When she reached the edge of the pool, she waved to Chef Claire and Josie, beamed at Max, and totally ignored me.

"Good morning, ladies," she said, sliding a lawn chair next to us and reaching out for the baby. "Hello, Sweetie. Come to grandma."

"She's wet, Mom," I said.

"She's fine," my mother said without looking at me as she held her arms out.

I handed Max to her and snuck a glance at Josie who merely shrugged.

"I take it you're still mad at me, Mom."

"Actually, I'm more disappointed," she said, totally focused on the baby.

"I'd prefer it if you were just mad, Mom."

"I know you would," she said, finally making eye contact. "But disappointment always seems to resonate better with you."

Josie and Chef Claire both laughed. I glared at both of them before turning back to my mother.

"Are you sure you can take Max for the day?"

"Of course," she said, cradling Max to her chest as she got to her feet.

"I laid out a fresh set of clothes for her," I said. "They're on the couch inside."

"That won't be necessary," she said, gently bouncing the baby in her arms. "I went shopping for her yesterday and have several new outfits for her to try on. We'll be fine. Won't we, Max?"

The baby gurgled and grabbed my mother's nose.

"Thanks, Mom. But you didn't need to do that. The kid has more clothes than I know what to do with."

"There's always room for more," she said, then spoke to Josie and Chef Claire. "What do you ladies have planned today?"

"I need to swing by the shelter," Josie said. "Then Chef Claire and I are having lunch at Veranda."

"Sounds wonderful," she said. "I love that restaurant."

"Aren't you going to ask me what I'm doing, Mom?"

"Actually, no," she said, wiping drool off Max's chin.

"I'm going to fix this, Mom."

"Hmmm. I'm tingling with anticipation."

I was about to snap back at her, but I caught Josie shaking her head, silently commanding me to let it go.

"Okay, you two have fun," I said, stroking Max's head. "I'll pick her up before five."

"Take all the time you need," my mother said. "Okay, we'll be off now."

We watched her stroll across the lawn until she disappeared through the gate.

"I've never seen her like that before," Chef Claire said. "How does it feel to be ghosted by your own mother?"

"Yeah, this is a bad one," I said. "But like I told her, I'm going to fix it."

"Hmmm," Josie said, doing her best impression of my mother. "I'm tingling with anticipation. How about you, Chef Claire?"

"Actually, I think I do feel a slight tingle in my legs," she said.

"You guys are no help," I said, stroking Chloe's head before firing a tennis ball the length of the pool where the other house dogs were fighting over a rope toy.

"Suzy," Josie said, turning serious. "You know how you're always talking about how your neurons have a tendency to take over and dominate your thoughts?"

"It rings a bell."

"You might want to consider letting them finish their work the next time before you jump in with both feet," Josie said.

"Thanks for the advice, Grasshopper," I said, making a face at her.

"I'm serious, Suzy. Just try to relax and roll with the punches, okay?"

"Where's the fun in that?" I said, then headed for the house to shower and change.

Chapter 10

Moral certitude is a concept I've never struggled with. I consider myself basically a right versus wrong type of person. But I'm well aware that stark black and white choices can be quite rare. And from time to time, most of us use misdirection and attempt to obfuscate issues and dilemmas we're facing, or, like now in my case, lie through our teeth to avoid hurting people's feelings and protect the ones we love. And despite the fact Gerald had seen fit to *keep a little* of the fifty million for himself, I had to weigh that against the benefits the hospital had provided to local residents. In the end, the choice to keep my mouth shut about the anonymous nature of the donation was an easy one. But to accomplish my goal, I would have to open my mouth at least one more time.

And lie through my teeth in the process.

"Hey, knock it off, Captain," I said, taking a few steps away from the water's edge when the Newfie decided standing next to me was the perfect spot to shake. But I hadn't seen him in time and ended up soaked by the time he was done. He sat down on his haunches and cocked his head at me. "You're lucky you're cute."

The Newfie woofed once at me then trotted to rejoin the other dogs who were fighting over the same stick. Since my mom was watching Max all day, and Josie and Chef Claire had left the house, I'd decided to bring the dogs with me to my lunch appointment. It had been a while since I had the dogs to myself, and I realized how much I'd missed spending time with them basically doing nothing. Chloe emerged from the sixteen-legged fur ball with the stick and proudly approached and dropped it at my feet. I laughed when I saw the expectant look on her face. When I didn't pick it up to throw it, she barked and pawed the sand with her front legs.

"No way. That's disgusting," I said, shaking my head at her. But when she barked a second time, I relented and threw the stick as far as I could downwind. All four dogs tore after it, and I used the brief respite to wipe the water off my face. My phone chirped, and I turned my back to the wind and hunched down with the phone pressed tight against my ear. "This is Suzy."

"Hey, it's me," Agent Tompkins said. "Sorry I couldn't take your call. I was in a meeting."

"No problem," I said, repositioning myself to block more of the stiff breeze.

"What's up?"

"I found the fifty million," I said. "So, you guys can stop looking for it."

"Actually, Suzy," the FBI agent said with a laugh. "We really hadn't gotten around to even start looking."

"Yeah, I get it," I said, nodding to myself. "You must have a ton of bigger problems to deal with."

"As a matter of fact, we do," he said. "Today's topic is gang violence."

"Where?"

"Where? How about pretty much every major city and town in the country."

"Got it. That's a big job. But I know you guys will figure it out."

"Thanks, Coach," he said, obviously anxious for me to get the conversation started. "Did you call to give me a pep talk or tell me about the missing fifty million?"

"Yeah, sorry," I said, watching the dogs who were back in the water and tugging at the stick. "Like I said, I found out what happened to the money."

"Well, don't keep me in suspense, Suzy. Spill."

"It was donated and used to build a hospital down here," I said, going for casual.

"That sounds like a good use for illegal drug money," Agent Tompkins said. "Who made the donation?"

"It was anonymous. But I asked my mother about it, and she's heard rumors the money was donated by the president of the bank where Slash had his account."

"Did the guy develop a guilty conscience at some point?"

"No idea," I said.

"Is he still around?"

"No, he retired soon after that. Nobody seems to know where he went. Or if he's even still alive."

"Okay, mystery solved. One less thing to worry about, right?"

"So, you're gonna cross it off your list?"

"Suzy, it was twenty years ago. At that time, I was still dealing with a severe case of acne and wondering if I'd ever find a girlfriend," he said, laughing. "Hey, the money was used to build a hospital. Why would I care who made the donation?"

"Yeah, that makes sense," I said with a grin.

"How's the murder investigation going? Not that I really care about that either."

"I'm not sure," I said. "I'm pretty much staying out of it."

"Yeah, and I'm the King of Scotland," Agent Tompkins deadpanned. "Is there anything else? I really need to get back to my meeting."

"No, that's it," I chirped. "Just thought you'd want to know."

"Thanks for calling. Talk to you soon."

He ended the call and I slid my phone into my shorts. I made a mental note to update Gerald and my mother at some point during the day, then headed for the water's edge to herd the dogs into some semblance of order.

"Okay, guys. Let's go," I called out. "We're gonna be late for lunch. Who wants a snack?"

The question, as always, worked its magic and the dogs immediately lost interest in the stick and clamored out of the water and raced toward me.

"No," I said, raising both arms to shield my face. A deluge washed over me, and when I opened my eyes, all four dogs were staring up at me. "Ahh, yuk. Thanks a lot. Let's go. Follow me."

I led the way across the small stretch of sand that led to a beachside café where I was meeting Detective Renfro for lunch. I spotted him sitting at an outside table studying a menu. When he saw me and the dogs, he waved then refocused on possible lunch choices. I sat down at the table, and he frowned when he got a close look at me.

"You just get out of the shower?"

"In a fashion," I said, nodding at the dogs who were all vying for the detective's attention. "Easy guys."

"No, they're fine," he said, taking time to pet all four. "They certainly have a great life down here."

"They have a great life regardless of location. They're incredibly spoiled," I said, shaking my head at the dogs. "I blame Josie." I laughed at my own joke, then lowered my voice. "Okay, settle. Who wants a snack?"

The dogs did as instructed and stared up at our server when she approached the table.

"Hi, Suzy," she said. "You brought the dogs. That's great. Normally, I'd pet them, but I think I might wait until they dry off a bit."

"Good call. How are you doing, Yvette?"

She spread her arms to take in the expansive view of the ocean and beamed at me.

"I could be doing a lot worse," she said. "What are you guys having for lunch?"

"Well, I'm gonna start with four burgers. No bun," I said.

"You doing a low carb thing?" Detective Renfro said, then smiled at our server.

"They're for the dogs, Smart Guy," I said, making a face at him.

"Four burgers for the bruisers. Got it," she said, scribbling on her pad. "What about you?"

"A burger. Medium," I said. "With fries. And an iced tea, please."

"You got it. Detective?"

"What the heck, let's make it easy. I'll have the same," he said, handing his menu to her.

"Okay, let me go put that order in."

I noticed the confused look on the dogs' faces and laughed.

"Hang on. It's coming."

"So," Detective Renfro said, sitting back in his chair and getting down to business. "There I am sitting at my desk this morning, and out of the blue, my buddy Suzy calls to invite me to lunch."

"You sound suspicious," I said. "Can't someone just invite a friend to lunch?"

"They can," he said with a shrug. "And I'm always delighted to eat free food. But usually, when you call, you want something."

"I'm going to ignore the cheap shot, Detective," I said, then leaned forward and placed both elbows on the table. "But now that you mention it, how's the murder investigation going?"

He laughed and shook his head at me.

"Unbelievable."

"Hey, some people like to chat about the weather. I'm more into talking about crime. And evildoers."

"Evildoers, huh? Well, to answer your question, there is no murder investigation."

Surprised, I sat back in my chair, and both Goldens seized their opportunity and plopped their heads in my lap. I gently scratched their ears as I formulated my next question. It was a simple choice.

"Why not?"

"Because we have no proof the guy was murdered," Detective Renfro said, then swigged from a bottle of water.

"But Paulie is convinced otherwise," I said,

"Yes, I'm sure he is," the detective said with a small shrug. "Unfortunately, when it comes to which cases we're going to pursue, Paulie doesn't get a vote."

"I didn't know the police were running a democracy," I said with a blank stare.

"We're not," he said, laughing. "But I'm sure you get my point."

"Your bosses don't want to investigate it?"

"My bosses…as you put it, don't believe there's anything to investigate."

"Do you?" I said, continuing to rub the Goldens' heads who were drifting off for a quick nap.

"No, actually I don't," Detective Renfro said, sitting back and smiling at the waitress who'd arrived with our drinks. "Thanks, Yvette."

"No problem. Your lunches will be right out."

When our server was out of earshot, he continued.

"Suzy, we have a suicide note, no visible signs of injury, and no indication anyone had a motive to kill the guy."

"Did you at least go out to Quiver's place?"

"We did. It's a nice house. Great view of the ocean."

"And?"

"And all we found were his personal belongings…including his will," Detective Renfro said.

"You found the will," I said, nodding. "Was it hard to find?"

"No, it was propped up on his laptop. Just sitting there in plain sight."

"So, he wanted to make sure you found it?" I said, rubbing my forehead before placing my hand back on Dente's head.

"It certainly looked like it," the detective said.

"Did you read it?"

"Of course, I read it," he said, frowning at me.

"Okay, relax. I'm just asking," I said, again massaging my forehead. "What did it say?"

"He left everything to his foundation," Detective Renfro said.

"Foundation? That's interesting. Does this foundation have a name?"

"The Quiver Society."

"Huh, sounds like a name for a group of nervous cats," I said, staring out at the ocean. "Who do they give their money to?"

"The description is a little fuzzy. And very broad. Basically, it talks about improving the life and lot of needy individuals."

"Did you find any of the Foundation's financials or annual reports?" I said.

"We're still digging into it," Detective Renfro said. "But since there's no murder investigation..."

"You're in no hurry to find it," I said, nodding. "Got it."

I took another look at the water, deep in thought.

"I smell something burning," he deadpanned.

"Funny," I said, then the nagging thought cleared when I remembered Agent Tompkins' question. "Did the handwriting you found on the documents at his place match the suicide note?"

"Perfectly," he said. "They were all written by the same guy. And that guy was definitely Little Billy Quiver."

"What was the date on the will?" I said, quickly running out of steam. And questions.

"Last week," he said, raising an eyebrow.

"A week ago? He was getting his house in order before he did it."

"That's our take. Now, do you understand why my superiors refused to open an investigation?"

"I do," I said. "Given the circumstances, I probably would have done the same thing."

"But it's still bugging you, right?"

"Yeah, I don't know why. But something is definitely nagging at me," I said, then gently slid both Goldens off my lap when I spotted our server heading our way carrying a large tray. "Maybe lunch will help."

"Here we go," Yvette said, setting the tray on the edge of the table. "Burgers for all."

"Great. I'm starved," I said, making room in front of me before accepting the dogs' plate.

"Do you need anything else at the moment?" she said.

"No, I think we're good," Detective Renfro said. "Thanks, Yvette."

She headed off after taking a few moments to pet all four dogs who were on point and fixated on the plate of burgers.

"You want to help?" I said.

"Sure," he said. "What do I do?"

"Just call Captain and Chloe to you," I said, breaking off a piece of one of the burgers. "Alternate pieces between both of them. You shouldn't have to worry about them sitting down, but if they give you any trouble, just stop feeding them until they do. And when you're done, just say 'That's all. Go lie down.'"

"Sounds easy," he said, reaching for one of the burgers. "They're incredibly well-behaved."

"Yeah, they're great," I said, glancing around with pride at all four.

"You could learn a thing or two from them," he said, laughing.

"You're a real hoot, Detective," I said, feeding both Goldens. "Feed your animals first."

"What?"

"Oh, it's something Rooster likes to say. It's actually great advice."

"How's he doing?"

"He's great," I said with a grin.

"Is he going to make it down here this winter?"

"No, Rooster's in love," I said, my grin widening.

"And being in love prevents him from traveling?"

"No, what's keeping him close to home this winter is who he's in love with," I said.

"Who might that be?"

"The new vet we hired last year to help Josie out and manage our wild animal sanctuary," I said. "And one of the major reasons we brought her on was to provide coverage at the Doggy Inn while we're down here."

"That's right," Detective Renfro said, holding out a piece of burger Captain gently took from his hand. "Josie was telling me you guys had started a sanctuary. How's that going?"

"It's good. But I think we're going to have to get rid of our elephant," I said, frowning. "She's becoming a real handful, and the poor thing struggles a bit with the cold weather."

Moments later, it was our turn to eat, and I attacked my burger with a vengeance. We ate in silence, and I watched a powerboat make its way across the water a couple hundred yards offshore. Another question popped.

"The boat that was anchored offshore when we found Quiver's body," I said.

"What about it?"

"Was it his?"

"It was not," Detective Renfro said, wiping his mouth.

"Who owned it?"

"I have no idea," he said, shrugging. "But it definitely didn't belong to Quiver."

"How do you know?"

"Because Quiver left a folder of all his belongings next to the will. And there was nothing there about him owning a powerboat. He had a fifty-foot sailboat."

"Where's the sailboat now?"

"We think he must have had it moored on another island or back in the States somewhere," Detective Renfro said.

"He was down here without his boat?"

"It looks that way," he said, focusing on his fries. "It'll turn up. And then I imagine it'll be sold and the proceeds will go to the Foundation."

"But who's going to handle that?" I said, puzzled.

"How the hell do I know?" he said, starting to run out of patience. "Geez, Suzy. Who do I look like? Foundation Man?"

"There's no need to get snarky," I snapped. "I'm just asking."

"And asking and asking and asking," he said, grinning at me. "Suzy, the guy killed himself, and I'd be surprised if there weren't a few loose ends and logistical problems to deal with."

"But he didn't have any family," I said.

"He must have at least had a board of directors at his foundation," Detective Renfro said. "Somebody will turn up at some point and handle all the issues. If there's money involved, trust me, somebody will come looking for it."

"Yeah, I'm sure you're right," I said, popping a couple of fries. "Have you talked to Samantha?"

"I have," he said. "She called this morning."

"What's she up to?"

"Well, she's pretty preoccupied with her new dog at the moment," he said. "But she called to get final confirmation it was okay to proceed with Little Billy's cremation."

"Cremation? Already?"

"Why not?" Detective Renfro said.

"It just seems really quick," I said, dredging a fry in ketchup.

"It was the first item on his will," he said, then recited from memory. "If you're reading this, it means I'm gone. My first request is I be cremated as soon as possible after my death and have my ashes scattered across the ocean."

"It sounds like the guy was very organized," I said. "Like he knew what needed to be taken care of before he went."

"Yeah, that's our take as well," he said.

"Then I guess there's nothing else to do but let it go," I said, then popped the last bite of my burger. "Hey, we're having dinner at the restaurant tonight. You want to join us? Gerald's going to be there. And I imagine having dinner with the Premier couldn't hurt your career goals, right?"

"I'm sure it couldn't," he said. "Thanks, but I can't make it. My wife is going to need a bit of a break tonight. She hasn't been getting enough sleep."

"You're a good guy, Detective Renfro," I said, wiping my mouth.

"Thanks," he said, laughing. "I'm glad you approve."

"It's a compliment," I said, making a face at him. "Just take it, okay?"

"Will do," he said. "What are you going to do now?"

"What do you mean?"

"Well, since the murder case didn't pan out, how are you going to keep yourself busy?"

"I have Max," I said. "She's more than enough to keep me busy."

"Try having four of them."

"Not a chance," I said, shaking my head. "You guys must be done having kids, right?"

"Not at all. We're going to take a bit of a break, but we're shooting for eight. We both come from large families."

"Geez," I said, overwhelmed by the prospect of having eight kids. "Well, if they keep coming two at a time, it shouldn't take you long. Hey, maybe you'll get lucky the next time and have quads."

"You sound like my wife," Detective Renfro said.

"She must be exhausted," I said. "Does she have any help?"

"Well, she's got me," he said. "For what that's worth."

"But you must be worn out as well by the time you get home from work."

"Sure," he said. "I'd like to be able to get a housekeeper to help out, but it's not in the cards at the moment."

"Maybe something will turn up," I said, then reached for the check Yvette had placed on the table.

Chapter 11

I swiveled halfway around on my stool and glanced around the packed dining room. I turned back and nudged Josie, who was sitting next to me slowly working her way through a glass of wine.

"You think it's too early to nominate Chef Claire for sainthood?" I said, nodding at the crowd while taking a sip of Pinot Grigio.

"The Church of the Full Belly?" Josie deadpanned.

"Yeah, that works," I said. "I doubt if the Catholics would be interested."

"Well, if she offered to serve the Rustic during Communion, it would have to help with attendance, right?"

"There you go," I said, laughing. "What did you guys do today?"

"We had lunch, did a bit of shopping, then caught a matinee."

"What did you see?"

"Some awful sci-fi thing," Josie said. "Ten minutes in, I got frigging lost trying to follow it. But the snacks saved the day. What about you?"

"I had lunch with Detective Renfro," I said. "Quiver's case has officially been listed as suicide. No murder investigation."

"I guess Paulie got it wrong," she said, then waved to the bartender for another round.

"Yeah, it looks like it," I said, then lowered my voice. "And I also managed to fix my screwup."

"How did you do that?" she said, leaning in close.

"I called Agent Tompkins and told him I found out what happened to the fifty million."

"And?"

"And the whole matter is officially off his list," I said.

"Well done," she said, gently punching me on the shoulder. "Have you told your mom and Gerald yet?"

"No, I thought it would be better doing it face to face over dinner," I said.

"Just so you can see mom's reaction, right?"

"Nothing gets past you," I said, laughing. "I doubt if she'll apologize for blowing up at me, but it should end the funk she's in."

"Well, we're gonna find out soon," Josie said, nodding at the front door where my mom, along with Paulie and Gerald, were chatting and laughing with the hostess.

I glanced down at Max, who was sitting contentedly on my lap sucking on a bottle of milk.

"Grandma's here, Sweetie. You ready for dinner?"

"You're a little late, aren't you?" Josie said, nodding at the bottle.

"Figure of speech," I said, sliding off my stool. "Let's get this over with."

We headed for the rest of our party, exchanged greetings, then I handed Max to Josie before pulling my mother in for a hug she stiffly accepted.

"Hi, Mom," I chirped. "You still mad at me?"

"Take a wild guess," she said through narrowed eyes.

"Well, be prepared to get rid of all that anger," I said, leading everyone to our table. "I have news."

"What on earth have you done now?" my mother said, directly behind me.

"Hold your horses," I said, taking Max back from Josie and working with our server to make sure she was secured in her high chair. Then I handed the bottle back to her, and she immediately began sucking in silence while glancing around the dining room. Then I sat down and took a sip of wine.

"What's your big news?" my mother said, not looking up from her menu.

"I fixed the problem," I said.

My mother set her menu down and glanced at Gerald and Paulie before focusing on me.

"Go on," she said softly.

I gave everyone at the table the short version of my conversation with Agent Tompkins. When I finished, I sat back and waited for questions.

"You told him the bank president was the one who donated the money for the hospital?" my mother said. "And you used my name as the source of the rumor?"

"Given the situation, I didn't think you'd mind," I said.

"No, that's fine," she said. "I can certainly handle that. Are you sure Agent Tompkins bought the story?"

"I'm positive. He hadn't even started looking into it. I think he was happy to be able to cross it off his list. He said twenty years was a long time, and since the money was used to build a hospital, it was no skin off his nose."

"Well done, darling," my mother said, patting my hand.

"So, you're not mad at me anymore?"

"Let's not get ahead of ourselves," she said, then patted my hand again.

"Did my name come up?" Gerald said.

"It did not," I said, grinning at him. "I laid everything on the bank president and told Agent Tompkins the guy pretty much disappeared after he retired."

"Which is basically true," Gerald said.

"I'm sorry I screwed up, Gerald," I said. "I'd never do anything to hurt you or your career."

"I know you wouldn't, Suzy."

"Just remember to keep your mouth shut in the future, darling," my mother said.

"I'm gonna let you have that one, Mom," I said, then beamed at her when the table broke up in laughter. Then I remembered my other conversation from earlier in the day and turned to Paulie.

"I had lunch with Detective Renfro today," I said to him.

"And?"

"And Quiver's death has been officially classified as a suicide," I said. "No murder investigation."

"They're making a mistake," Paulie said, shaking his head.

"They don't have anything to investigate," I said.

"It doesn't appear they looked very hard."

"Stuff happens," Gerald said, studying his menu.

"Hey, where's your entourage, Gerald? There's usually at least a couple people hovering around you."

"I gave them the night off," he said, reaching for his wine glass. "And they know where to find me."

"I'd hate having to deal with that," Josie said.

"It does get old," Gerald said. "But it comes with the territory."

"Another perk of office?" I said with a grin.

"Don't start, darling," my mother snapped. "You just managed to get yourself out of the hole. Let's not start by digging another, okay?"

"Whatever you say, Mom," I said softly.

"Somebody write that down," my mother said to the table. "I'm not sure I'll ever hear that again.

Another round of laughter ensued at my expense, but I wasn't going to let anything ruin my good mood. Halfway through dinner, Chef Claire emerged from the kitchen and headed straight for our table.

"How is everything?" she said, glancing around.

"Trick question, right?" Josie said, sliding a piece of grilled fish into her mouth.

"I wasn't talking to you," Chef Claire said. "You'd eat a car bumper if I put enough butter on it."

"Everything's wonderful, dear," my mother said. "As always."

"Thanks, Mrs. C."

"I've been meaning to ask you, Chef Claire," Gerald said. "I'm throwing a dinner party next week for some visiting dignitaries at my place and was wondering if I could talk you into catering it?"

"I don't know, Gerald," she said, shaking her head. "That's asking a lot. And this is supposed to be my time away from work."

"But you're here every time I come to the restaurant," Gerald said.

"Which kinda proves my point," she said. "How many people?"

"No more than a dozen."

"Let me check with the kitchen staff and see if they can fit it in," she said.

"Perfect," Gerald said. "Thank you."

"I'll let you know as soon as I can," she said, then nodded at the front door where two uniformed policemen were talking to the hostess. "I wonder what they want."

Both cops turned in our direction, then headed straight for the table.

"I think we're about to find out," Josie said, wiping her mouth.

The police officers came to a stop next to Gerald, who stared up at them with a puzzled look on his face. They appeared sheepish and tentative, two traits I didn't often use to describe cops.

"We're so sorry to interrupt your dinner, Premier," one of the cops said.

"Yes, we're very sorry, sir," the other cop said, nervously shifting back and forth on his feet.

"How can I help you?" Gerald said.

"I'm afraid we're going to have to ask you to come outside with us," the first cop said.

"Outside? What on earth for?"

"Perhaps we should wait to discuss that until we're outside, Premier."

"Officer," Gerald said, then leaned forward until he could read his nametag. "Officer Givens. I'm only halfway through my dinner and am not going anywhere until I know what this is about. Am I making myself clear?"

"Absolutely, Premier," the cops said, taking several deep breaths. "Okay, we need you to come with us because of an anonymous tip we received earlier."

"An anonymous tip about what?" Gerald said, his voice rising.

"We need to look in the trunk of your car, Premier," the second cop said.

"My trunk?" Gerald said, thoroughly confused. "Why do you need to look in my trunk?"

The cops glanced at each other, apparently deciding which one of them was going to break the news. Then Officer Givens nodded and stared at Gerald.

"We've been told there's something in your trunk that may need some explanation."

"That is an unfounded rumor," Gerald snapped.

"I'm sorry, sir. I'm not following you," Officer Givens said.

"I paid for those clubs. They were in no way a gift from the Swiss Consulate."

"What?" the cop said with a deep frown.

"My golf clubs," Gerald said. "What else would you be talking about? They're the only thing in my trunk at the moment." He glanced around the table. "A lot of good they do me. I haven't been able to get a round in for months."

"We do need to get out," Paulie said.

"No, sir," Officer Givens said. "We're not talking about your golf clubs. But if you could come outside with us, I'm sure we can clear this up in no time."

"Fine," Gerald said, tossing his napkin on the table and getting to his feet. Then he spotted me also getting up. "You want to tag along?"

"Actually, I do," I said. "Color me intrigued."

"Yeah, I wouldn't mind taking a look," Josie said.

"Then let's all go," Gerald said, motioning for everyone to join in. "That way, you'll all have a birds-eye view when you witness these two gentlemen's careers take a giant step backward."

"Chef Claire," I said. "Do you mind keeping an eye on Max for a few minutes?"

"Not the briar patch," Chef Claire, then bent down and lifted Max into her arms. "And how was your dinner?"

Max gurgled and giggled and grabbed Chef Claire's nose.

"Thanks," I said, following Gerald to the door.

Outside, Gerald led the way to his car which was parked in front. He reached the back of the car, grabbed his keys from his pocket and opened the trunk. All of us stared in disbelief at the sight that greeted us.

"What the hell?" Gerald whispered.

"Oh, no," I said, my eyes immediately welling with tears. "Not Samantha."

"Who's Samantha?" Gerald said with a wild-eyed stare.

"She's the medical officer who's taking over for Jimmy while he's on vacation," I said.

"She was," Josie said, shaking her head at the body stuffed in the trunk.

"What is going on?" Gerald said, reaching down to touch the body.

"No, Premier," Officer Givens said. "Don't touch the body."

"What on earth is she doing in my trunk?" Gerald said, stunned.

"We're hoping you might be able to explain it to us, sir," the second cop said.

"You really don't think I had anything to do with this, do you?"

"For now, let's just say you need to come with us so we can discuss it," Officer Givens said.

"What?" Gerald said.

"Just do what they say, Gerald," my mother said. "We'll be right behind you. Should I call Xavier?"

"What? Oh, Xavier," Gerald said, shaking his head as if clearing the cobwebs away. "Yes, you should probably call him. Have him meet me at the police station." He took one more look at Samantha's body, then focused on the cops. "Okay, let's go."

"Those won't be necessary," my mother said, nodding at the pair of handcuffs Officer Givens was about to put on Gerald. "Show some respect."

"I'm sorry, ma'am," the cop said. "Standard protocol."

"Standard protocol for your common street thug," my mother snapped. "That's the Premier you're about to handcuff."

"Trust me, Mrs. C., I'm very aware of who it is and what I'm about to do. I'm sorry, but I'm afraid I'm going to have to insist," Officer Givens said.

"Do it, and you'll regret it the rest of your life," my mother said, giving the cop her best death stare. Even though I wasn't the target, it still sent a chill up my spine.

"I know you have a lot of juice down here, Mrs. C., but I'm afraid you don't get a vote in this matter," Officer Given said.

I had to give him credit. He was hanging tough.

"You wanna bet your annual salary on that?" my mother said.

"I beg your pardon?"

"A little wager. About whether I get a vote or not," she said. "Let me ask you a question, Officer Givens."

"Okay," he said, puzzled.

"How do you like your new headquarters?" my mother said.

"Headquarters? It's great," he said with a shrug.

"Who do you think had it built?" my mother said.

"I just assumed it was part of the government's budget," he said.

"Do me a favor," my mother said. "When you get to the station, ask the Chief. And if Gerald is handcuffed when you bring him in, I'll be the least of your concerns. Am I being clear...Officer Givens?"

The cops glanced nervously each other, then Officer Givens shrugged.

"I guess he's not an escape threat. Okay, no cuffs."

"Thank you, Officer Givens," my mother said, softening. "Gerald, we'll be right behind you. Paulie, would you mind driving? I'm a bit preoccupied at the moment."

"No problem," Paulie said, giving Gerald a quick hug before heading off.

We watched Gerald climb into the back of the police car. He sat quietly in the back seat as the two cops chatted briefly with each other. Then Officer Givens climbed in behind the wheel and drove off. The other officer approached Gerald's car and closed the trunk.

"If you don't mind stepping away from the car, they'll be a lot of people showing up soon. And I'm sorry about the disruption to the restaurant."

I got one final quick peek at Samantha's body before the cop managed to close the trunk. I brushed my tears away with the back of my hand, then gave my mother a quick embrace before she climbed into the passenger seat of her SUV. They headed off and Josie and I sat down on the top step of the entrance.

"Wow," Josie whispered. "It looks like she got shot in the back of the head."

"Yeah."

"Why would anybody want to kill Samantha?" she whispered.

"I have no idea," I said. "But I was right about something."

"What's that?"

"Somebody is trying to set Gerald up for murder. I just had the wrong victim."

"What a mess," she said.

"Oh, no," I said.

"What is it?"

"The Weimaraner," I said, reaching for my phone.

"Who are you calling?"

"Detective Renfro. We need to get out to Jimmy's place and grab the dog."

"Good call. What was the term you used to describe Ruby?"

"Whimsical," I said, waiting for the call to connect.

"I wonder if that's going to last," Josie said.

"What?"

"The poor thing has lost two owners in a couple of days. There's nothing whimsical about that."

Chapter 12

I sat up on my lounge chair when I saw my mom's headlights appear in her driveway. It was after two, but Josie and I were still up and sitting poolside sipping coffee. Chef Claire had arrived home exhausted and had gone straight to bed after we gave her an update about what we knew, which wasn't much. Max had gone down without protest, and we hadn't heard a peep out of her. Chloe had staked out her usual spot next to Max's crib, while Al and Dente had followed Chef Claire inside the house and were undoubtedly sacked out, sprawled across her bed taking up way too much room. Captain, unwilling to leave Josie's side until she turned in, was spread out over a beach towel and snoring loudly at the edge of the pool.

We smiled as we listened to the loud, rhythmic pattern of Captain's snores.

"Remember how little he was when you got him?" I said, nodding at the Newfie.

"Yeah, that didn't last long," Josie said, giving the dog a loving stare. "You want to head over to your mom's place and get an update?"

"Nah, I'm sure she's worn out. It can wait until morning," I said, then spotted the outside gate that led down to the beach swing open. "Or maybe it can't."

Captain heard the gate open and hopped to his feet. A guttural growl emerged and began to build until he realized who the visitor was. Then his tail started wagging, and he trotted across the lawn to greet my mother.

"Hi, Mom," I said, dragging a chair between the two loungers.

"I saw the lights on and thought I'd stop by. I'm still too keyed up to sleep."

"You want some coffee?"

"No, thanks," she said, sitting down. "But I wouldn't say no to a little bourbon on the rocks."

"Bourbon at two in the morning?" I said, getting up to fix her drink. "You have had a long night."

"Indeed," she said, rubbing Captain's head.

"Did Paulie go to bed?" Josie said.

"Yeah, he's worn out," my mother said, accepting the glass I was holding out. "Thanks, darling."

She took a small sip, then another larger one.

"This is one of those nights when I wished I still smoked," she said, laughing.

"Well, don't keep us in suspense," I said, settling back into the lounger.

"He was released on his own recognizance about a half-hour ago."

"Any bail?" Josie said.

"No, not yet."

“So, they didn’t charge him?” I said.

“No. For obvious reasons, they’re holding off until they have a bit more information,” my mother said.

“A dead body in his trunk wasn’t enough?” Josie said.

“I guess that makes sense,” I said, stifling a yawn. “Charging the Premier with murder prematurely probably isn’t the best career move.”

“Yeah, premature charging is the worst,” Josie deadpanned.

My mother laughed, and I looked over and shook my head at Josie.

“Don’t start,” I said, stifling a laugh. “Did you get a chance to talk with Gerald?”

“We did,” my mother said. “He’s rattled.”

“I’m sure he is,” I said. “Does he have any idea how the body could have got there?”

“No, according to Gerald, the car hadn’t left his garage all day. And the first time he was in it today was when he drove to the restaurant.”

“That’s right,” I said, remembering another of Gerald’s perks of office. “He has a driver who takes him everywhere.”

“Yes,” my mother said. “Including to and from his office.”

“But if the car hadn’t been out of the garage, that means someone must have broken in and put the body there during the day.”

“Nothing gets past you,” Josie said.

"Shut it. I'm merely talking out loud to help me formulate my theory," I said, making a face at her.

"And?"

"And I'm still formulating," I said.

"Well, it is after two, so I guess I'll have to cut you some slack," Josie said, laughing as she got to her feet. "But I'm beat. I'm going to bed."

"See you in the morning," I said.

"Goodnight, dear," my mother said.

"You mind checking in on Max before you go to bed?"

"Already number one on my list," she said, then whistled softly. Captain lifted his head off the beach towel. "You ready for bed, Goofball?"

Captain hopped to his feet and led the way into the house.

"You want a top-up, Mom?" I said, nodding at her glass.

"No, I'm good," she said, stretching out in Josie's lounger.

"What did Gerald have to say? You know, does he have any idea who might be trying to set him up?"

"Not directly. But it has to be someone who was involved with Little Billy Quiver, right?"

"Some sort of attempt to frame Gerald while trying to find the missing fifty million?" I said, frowning. "I suppose it's possible. But it sounds like a bit of a stretch, Mom."

"Well, maybe Quiver was working with a partner. And after Little Billy removed himself from the equation, whoever it is decided the plan was too good to pass up. Fifty million is a lot of money."

"Even for you, huh?" I said, grinning at her.

"Yes, darling. Even for me."

"But why bother trying to set Gerald up if money was the primary motive?"

"That is a good question," she said, polishing off the last of her bourbon. "Maybe I will have one more."

She headed off to refresh her drink. I stared up at the night sky and tried to sort through the jumbled collection of thoughts rolling around my head. My mother settled back into her lounge chair, and we sat in silence for several moments.

"The only motive I can think of for why Gerald is being set up is revenge," I said softly.

"The letter Gerald received made that pretty clear," my mother said. "But since Little Billy is dead, how do you explain the revenge angle now?"

"Well, since he didn't have any family members, I think you're right about him working with a partner. Maybe a woman he was involved with. Over time, maybe she bought into the idea that Gerald was the one who ruined the old man's life. Maybe she thought it was up to her to continue Billy's plan to take Gerald down."

"Unless the two events aren't connected," my mother said with a shrug.

"Are you talking about one of Gerald's political enemies?"

"I am. He certainly has some."

"Wow," I said, surprised. "That's pretty good, Mom. Not a bad theory at all."

"Thank you, darling," she said, taking a small sip. "You don't think all your deductive powers simply fell from the sky, do you?"

I laughed.

"Yeah, I suppose I can blame you for some of that, can't I?"

"Blame isn't the word I would use."

"And if you're right, Samantha could have just been in the wrong place at the wrong time," I said. "If the plan were to set Gerald up for murder, it wouldn't matter who the victim was, right?"

"That's what I've been thinking, darling."

"And it was obvious Gerald didn't have a clue who Samantha was."

"No, he's adamant he'd never seen her before," my mother said.

"That could come in handy."

"Maybe," she said with a frown. "As long as no other evidence shows up."

"But either way, he's gonna take a political hit, isn't he?"

"Oh, you can count on it. I'm not sure he can survive something like this. Which would be a tragedy since he's doing some great work."

"Has the press got the story yet?"

"What do you think?" my mother said, glancing over. "The Premier gets pulled in on suspicion of murder. I imagine somebody leaked it as soon as Gerald entered the police station."

"Which supports your theory that it could be one of his political enemies," I said.

"Make sure you read the paper in the morning," my mother said. "It should be riveting."

"The poor guy," I said, shaking my head. "I love Gerald."

"Me too," she said, draining her drink. "What time do you want to drop Max off in the morning?"

"What?"

"You're going to need a sitter tomorrow."

"I am?" I said, confused.

"Yes. You're going to be very busy."

"Doing what?"

"Figuring out what the hell is going on around here, what else?"

"You're encouraging me to do some snooping?"

"Let's call it an order," my mother said, getting to her feet and leaning in close for a hug. "And don't screw this one up, darling. There's a lot riding on it."

"Wow," I said with a frown. "I think I've entered an alternate universe."

"Funny. Figure this thing out, darling. But remember, until we know a bit more, we can't trust anybody."

"Even the cops?"

“Especially the cops,” she said, then headed for home with an over the shoulder wave. But she stopped and turned back to me. “One more thing, darling. I will, of course, expect regular updates.”

“I knew there had to be a catch,” I called out as she continued the journey back to her house.

I sat quietly, deep in thought.

“Wow,” I whispered. “Permission. That’s gonna be weird.”

Chapter 13

Our first stop the next morning was Jimmy's house on the other side of town. It was early, and Josie and I were operating on too little sleep. But we were well stocked with steaming travel mugs of coffee, and traffic was mercifully light. I drove while Josie read the paper in the passenger seat. She occasionally grunted and grimaced as she read the page one article.

"How bad is it?" I said.

"About what you'd expect," she said, flipping to the next page where the story continued.

"Page one and two," I said, frowning. "That's not good."

"Well, it's certainly more newsworthy than anything else happening down here at the moment."

"Who wrote the article?"

"Geoffrey Jones," Josie said.

"That should help. He's usually in Gerald's corner."

"Yeah, he is. But there's not a lot of ways to spin this one," Josie said, then closed the paper and tossed it on the back seat. "Is Detective Renfro meeting us there?"

"He is," I said, slowing down to make a right turn.

"Did he put up a fight?"

"No, he's a dog guy. He said he'd drop everything and head right over," I said. "Hey, I got an idea."

"Already? You haven't even finished your coffee."

"Not about that," I said, pulling next to the curb in front of Jimmy's house. "About what to do with the Weimaraner."

"Do tell," Josie said as she climbed out of the SUV.

"Teresa's kids have been bugging her to get a dog. And they fell in love with Ruby at the party the other night. Let's check with Teresa then surprise the kids."

"I like it," Josie said, arching her back to stretch. Then she gave Detective Renfro a wave when his car pulled in directly behind ours. "Good morning."

"Good morning," the detective said. "Big news last night, huh?"

"Yeah," I said. "He didn't do it."

"Of course, he didn't," Detective Renfro said. "But it's bad."

"Are you hearing anything around the station?" I said.

"Nothing specific," he said, leading the way up the front steps. "Just a ton of rumor and chatter."

He slipped on a pair of latex gloves then removed a set of keys from his pocket and opened the front door.

"Where did you get the house key?" Josie said.

"Think about it," he said, then shook his head when he caught the blank stare on her face. "Samantha was house sitting, remember?"

"Oh," Josie said, chagrined. "Never mind."

We headed inside and came to a stop and looked around the living room. Seeing no signs of the dog, we continued working our way to the back of the house and calling the dog's name.

"I'll check the upstairs," Josie said.

"Don't touch anything," Detective Renfro said. "A couple of techs are on their way over."

"Got it," Josie said, then disappeared up the stairs.

Detective Renfro and I made our way in and out of the kitchen, then down the hall where two small bedrooms were located. Coming up empty, we headed back into the living room and sat down. Josie returned a few moments later.

"Nothing," she said.

"Where the heck did she go?" I said. "The house looks secure. And there's no way Samantha would have let her out to roam the neighborhood while she was at work." I looked over at Detective Renfro. "She didn't bring the dog with her to work by any chance, did she?"

"I doubt it," he said. "But we can easily find out."

"Maybe Samantha was grabbed here after work, and Ruby managed to get out while the door was open," I said.

"That works," Josie said. "Let's swing by the shelter and start getting the word out to be on the lookout."

"I'll put something out on the radio, too," the detective said. "Silver Weimaraner, right?"

"Yeah. Thanks," I said.

"Okay, you guys should get out of here," he said, glancing out the window. "I need to stick around until the techs show up. And then I've got a ton of other things to take care of. One, in particular, I am not looking forward to."

"Talking to Samantha's parents, right?" I said softly.

"Make that two things I'm not looking forward to," he said, shooing us out of the house with the back of his hand.

"See you soon," I said, heading for the door. "Hey, who's handling the examination of Samantha's body?"

"Jimmy," Detective Renfro said. "His flight lands this morning."

"He cut his vacation short?" I said, surprised.

"He did."

"Before or after he heard about Samantha's death?" I said.

"I don't have a clue. Does it matter?"

"Probably not," I said. "I was just wondering."

"Because that's what you do, right?" the detective said with a laugh.

"Don't worry," Josie said. "She's just getting started. And if you need to find us later, just follow the burning smell."

"Funny," I said, making a face at her.

"Let's go, Snoopmeister," she said, pointing at the SUV. "You promised to buy me breakfast."

***

"I ate too much," Josie said, frowning as she tugged at the waistband of her shorts.

"Really? I hadn't noticed."

"I noticed you didn't show much restraint, either," she said, stifling a burp.

"I'm stress eating," I said, staring out at the traffic that was beginning to build.

"That's a good excuse. I think I'll use it."

"You're welcome," I said, turning into the parking lot in front of the building where Jimmy's office was located.

I parked and we headed inside. Moments later, we were standing outside the office, and I knocked softly.

"Yeah," came the voice from inside. "Come on in."

We entered and closed the door behind us.

"Hey, Jimmy," I said.

"Suzy, nice to see you. Present circumstances notwithstanding. How are you doing, Josie?"

"I'm good," she said, then glanced around the office. "You know, present circumstances notwithstanding."

"Got it," he said, gesturing for us to sit down.

"I'm sorry you had to cut your vacation short," I said.

"Don't worry about it. I was already on my way back."

"You were?"

"Yeah, I landed for an interview in Chicago and was greeted by a foot of snow and a thirty mile an hour wind off the lake," Jimmy said, then took a sip of coffee.

"Yuk," I said, grimacing at the prospect of dealing with the northern winter. "I hope you were dressed for it."

"I had five layers on," he said, shaking his head. "And I was wearing a down parka that hundreds of geese must have died for."

"I take it that was enough to remove Chicago as a potential landing spot," Josie said.

"It was. Then I flew to L.A. for another interview and spent two hours in the car trying to go eight miles. Then I had an epiphany."

"That you were a total idiot for even thinking about leaving the island?" I said, laughing.

"Pretty much," he said. "I exited the highway, turned the rental around, and headed straight for the airport to catch the first flight back."

"I'm glad to hear it. I'm just sorry you had to come back to this mess."

"Yeah," he said, exhaling softly. "I liked Samantha. She's was a good woman."

"How well did you know her?"

"Pretty well," he said. "I met her at a conference a few years ago, and we stayed in touch. And she jumped at the chance to handle things down here while I was away. Life's choices. I guess you never know what's gonna happen, huh?"

"No, you don't. What time are her parents getting in?"

He raised an eyebrow at me, apparently surprised I knew about her parents' arrival, but let it pass without comment. "This afternoon. They're crushed."

"How could you not be? It's a horrible situation," I said softly. "All around."

"You don't think he did it, do you?" Jimmy said, rocking slowly in his chair.

"Gerald? No way," I snapped. "And you should know better than to even ask the question, Jimmy."

"They found her in his trunk, Suzy. It's a logical question to ask."

"He's being set up," I said.

"Who would want to do that?" Jimmy said.

"That seems to be the fifty-million-dollar question."

"What?"

"Nothing," I said. "Have you confirmed the cause of death?"

"Yup. Just like it looked. One nine-mil in the back of the head."

I exhaled loudly and felt my eyes well with tears. I sat quietly trying to compose myself before continuing. Then I spotted the urn sitting on his desk.

"What's that?"

"Those are the remains of Mr. William Quiver," he said, glancing briefly at the urn. He stopped rocking and draped a leg over his knee. "Quite a reminder, huh?"

"What?" I said, frowning.

"A reminder to live each day as if it were your last," he said, resuming his rocking. "Because in the end, we're all going to end up in either one of those, or buried in a hole in the ground."

"Now, there's a cheery thought," Josie deadpanned.

"Yeah," I said, nodding. "And I was just about to tell you how much I missed you, Jimmy."

"It's a pretty basic concept, guys," he said. "You live, you die, and the world keeps spinning without missing a beat."

"And he wonders why he has so much trouble getting a date," Josie said, laughing.

"Yeah," I said, grinning at her. "Lovely dinner conversation."

"Hey, if you spent your day the same way I do, trust me, you'd have the same take."

"I'll take your word for it," I said, ready to change topics. "What's going to happen to Quiver's ashes?"

"They'll be put in our storage until somebody shows up to claim them," he said.

"Has anybody called yet?" I said.

"Not that I know of," he said. "But I'm sure they will. Look, I've only been back a couple of hours, and I'm already way behind. Did you need something specific, or did you just drop by to chat?"

"We just wanted to confirm the cause of death," I said, getting to my feet. "We'll get out of your hair."

"One nine-mil in the back of the head," he said with a shrug. "And you can quote me on that."

"Okay," I said, extending my hand. "Stop by the restaurant when you get a chance. We'll treat you to a welcome home dinner."

"Thanks. I'll be there soon."

"Have a better one," Josie said, heading to the door with a small wave.

"Nice to see you, guys," he said. "Oh, Suzy. One more thing."

"What's that?" I said, turning around.

"Figure out who's behind this. Gerald doesn't deserve it."

"No, he doesn't," I said, opening the door and stepping into the hallway.

"Where to now, Sherlock?" Josie said.

"I thought we'd swing by Gerald's office," I said, heading off at a brisk pace.

"Hang on, Speed Racer," Josie said, quickening her pace. "Huh, how about that?"

"What?" I said, glancing over without slowing down.

"I'm having a hard time keeping up with you," she said, surprised. "Chef Claire has worked her magic. Maybe I should start running."

"Trust me," I said, shaking my head. "Jogging's overrated."

"Well, it's definitely working," she said. "You look great."

"Thanks," I said, beaming at her as I reached for my phone.

We stopped outside before heading to the car while I made the call. Gerald's executive assistant answered on the second ring.

"Premier's office," Marjorie said, her voice muted and tinged with despair.

"Hey, Marjorie. It's Suzy."

"Hi, Suzy," she said, then exhaled into the phone. "If you're looking for him, I'm afraid he's not here."

"Oh, no," I said, immediately concerned.

"What is it?" Josie said.

I waved her off and focused on the phone.

"No, he's fine," Marjorie continued. "He's working from home today. We thought he should keep a low profile until things quiet down a bit. The press is camped out in front of the building."

"Good call. Is he up for visitors?"

"I'm sure he'll make an exception for you."

"Cheap shot, Marjorie," I snapped.

"No, I wasn't taking a shot at you, Suzy," she said. "He needs help. And I know he trusts your abilities."

"Okay. I'm sorry I yelled at you," I said, rubbing my forehead.

"Don't worry about it. Just promise me you'll do everything you can to figure out what the hell is going on around here."

"Will do."

"I'll give him a call and let him know you're on your way," she said.

"Thanks, Marjorie. Tell him we'll be there in about fifteen minutes," I said, ending the call.

"And?" Josie said.

"Gerald's house," I said, pointing toward the SUV.

Chapter 14

Josie whistled softly when she spotted the house emerge at the top of the winding driveway.

"Wow," she whispered.

"Oh, that's right," I said, glancing over. "You've never been here before."

"No, I haven't," she said, staring out at the ornate landscaping. "And I have to ask, why not?"

"Gerald likes his privacy," I said with a shrug. "And apart from the occasional dinner party, I think he only brings certain women back to his house. If you get my drift."

"Got it. He paid a million bucks for this place twenty years ago?"

"Yeah," I said, coming to a stop in the circular drive.

"I wonder what it's worth now?" she said, climbing out of the SUV.

"More than one," I said, glancing around the house.

"Thanks for clarifying," she said, gently punching me on the shoulder. "Whoever said crime doesn't pay?"

"Whatever you do, please don't bring that up while we're here," I said, staring at her.

"What am I, an idiot?"

"We need to be supportive, yet gently inquisitive," I said by way of instruction.

"Got it," she said, heading for the stairs that led up to the house. "Nosy and annoying, it is."

"Funny," I said, ringing the doorbell.

We both turned around to admire the lawn while we waited.

"Nice, huh?" I said.

"I think it left nice in the rear-view mirror. This is incredible. It's good to be king, huh?"

"Get it all out of your system now," I said.

"Okay. I'm done," she said, grinning at me.

The door opened and Gerald poked his head out. He waved us in and closed the door behind us.

"Hi," he said, peering out the small window next to the door. "Did you see any media out there?"

"No," I said. "Marjorie said they're hanging out at your office."

"She told me," Gerald said, motioning for us to follow him down the hall to the atrium that led outside to the pool. "I'm sure they'll figure out soon enough I'm not there."

"Geez," Josie said as she gawked at the inside of the house. "This place is incredible, Gerald."

"Yeah, thanks, I like it," he said, continuing outside until we reached a poolside table. "But let's hope I'm not forced to start spending all my time here."

We sat down and he poured iced tea for us. Then he sat back in his chair and lit a cigar. He puffed until it was burning the way he wanted, then focused on me.

"What have you heard?"

"Not much," I said with a shrug. "We stopped by Jimmy's place this morning to pick up the Weimaraner and ran into Detective Renfro."

"He just called," Gerald said. "He's on his way over."

"Why?" I said, raising an eyebrow.

"To execute a search warrant," he said softly.

"They're looking for the murder weapon," I said.

"I'm sure they are," he said with a shrug. "Well, they can look all they want."

"Are you sure about that?"

"What are you talking about, Suzy?"

"If someone was able to break in and stuff Samantha's body in the trunk of your car, what makes you think they weren't able to plant the gun somewhere in the house?"

"Ah, crap," Gerald said, almost dropping his cigar. "I didn't even think about that."

"Well, you have been a bit preoccupied," Josie said.

"Should we take a look?" I said.

"There's no time," Gerald said, a deep frown etched on his face. "Detective Renfro said he was only about ten minutes away."

"Maybe you'll get lucky," I said, then a thought bubbled to the surface. "Did anything show up on your security system? I know you've got video surveillance."

"It was offline for a half-hour yesterday," Gerald said. "By the time I noticed the message on my phone, it came back on before I could call the security company. At the time, I figured it was just a glitch, or they were doing some maintenance work."

"So, they managed to bypass all your security," I said. "They're good. You've got state of the art technology here."

"I thought I did," he said. "You got any ideas about what the heck is going on?"

"I have a few vague notions. But nothing concrete."

"Well, I'd love to hear anything you come up with," he said, tapping the ash off his cigar.

"I think whoever was trying to set you up for Quiver, decided to change course after the cops wrote it off as a suicide," I said.

"Change course?" Gerald said.

"You know, up the ante," I said, shrugging. "If they couldn't pin Quiver on you, then their next option was to try the same strategy with a different person."

"But why would anybody want to kill that young woman?" Gerald said, shaking his head. "She had nothing to do with this situation."

"I know," I said. "Maybe they just needed a body, and she was the first one they came across."

"An opportunity killing?" Gerald said.

"It's certainly a possibility," I said.

I caught the frown on Josie's face.

"What is it?"

"I don't know," she said, shaking her head. "It seems too easy of an explanation. Maybe she was chosen because of the work she did."

I sat back in my chair and gave Josie's comment some serious thought.

"How so?" Gerald said, leaning forward.

"Maybe she discovered something about Quiver when she was working on his body," Josie said.

"Like what?" I said.

"How the hell do I know?" she said. "This is your area of expertise. I'm way out of my depth here."

Before I could respond, we heard the sound of the doorbell. Gerald set his cigar down then got to his feet.

"Okay," he said, running a hand through his hair. "Showtime."

We watched him head back inside the house then I spotted Josie waving cigar smoke away from her face.

"The wind's shifted," she said with a scowl. "You mind putting that thing out?"

"Gladly," I said, crushing out the cigar.

We sat in silence until Gerald returned trailed by Detective Renfro and the same two cops who'd been at the restaurant the previous evening. We exchanged perfunctory greetings, then Gerald focused on the detective.

"What do you need from me?" Gerald said.

"Nothing, sir," Detective Renfro said. "And again, I apologize for having to do this."

"I understand, Detective," he said, then turned to Josie and me. "Why don't we head up to the rooftop while the police do what they need to do?"

"Sure," I said, getting up from my chair.

Gerald led the way, and we trailed behind as he started up a long set of steps attached to the side of the house.

"Rooftop?" Josie whispered as we started our ascent.

"That's news to me," I said.

When we made it to the top, we were greeted by a magnificent view of the water. The terrace looked like it belonged more in a hotel lobby than it did on top of a house.

"Wow," Josie whispered.

"That's the word for it," I said, stunned. "Geez, Gerald. This is incredible."

"Thanks," he said, gesturing at several plush chairs and couches set amid a diverse collection of plants and flowers. "Cocktail?"

"I usually wait until the sun is all the way up," Josie deadpanned.

"Me too," Gerald said, grabbing a beer from the fridge. "But I'm going to make an exception today. You sure you won't join me?"

We both waved his offer off, then spotted the covered object at the same time.

"What's that?" I said.

"Oh, that's my telescope," he said. "I love watching the stars at night."

"And topless sunbathers during the day?" Josie said with a grin.

"I suppose it's been known to happen," he said, grinning back. "Check it out. It's amazing."

We walked over and Josie leaned in close to the eyepiece.

"It's all fuzzy," she said, glancing up at the Premier.

"Use the little gizmo next to your right hand," he said, then took a long sip of beer.

"There we go," she said, nodding. "You're right. It's incredible. I can look right into all the boats going by."

"Let me see," I said, then took Josie's spot when she took a step to the side. "Holy crap. This thing is amazing."

"It oughta be," Gerald said. "It cost me a small fortune."

I slowly moved the telescope back and forth as I continued to stare through the lens. Then my eyes landed on a boat heading out to sea, and I let loose with a loud shriek and jerked backward. Josie jumped back, startled.

"How many times do I have to tell you not to do that?" she snapped.

"Sorry. But you need to see this."

I moved away from the telescope, and she resumed her position.

"This better be good," she said, glaring as she glanced up. "What am I looking at?"

"The sailboat heading away from the island at about three o'clock," I said, pointing as my mind continued to race.

Josie looked through the lens then gasped.

"Do you see it?" I said.

"Standing near the back of the boat?" Josie said.

"Is that who I think it is?"

"Yeah, I'd recognize her anywhere," she said.

"Who is it?" Gerald said, heading for the telescope.

"It's Ruby," I whispered.

"Who the hell is Ruby?" he said, bending down and adjusting the eyepiece.

"The Weimaraner," I said, staring out to sea at the boat that was rapidly becoming a distant speck.

"Okay," Josie said. "I'm officially confused."

"Is there a name on the back of the boat?" I said to Gerald who continued to look through the telescope.

"Yeah," he said, without taking his eyes off the boat. "Wanderlust. It's registered down here."

"How do you know that?" Josie said.

"Because it says Grand Cayman right below the name," Gerald said.

"Oh, I did not see that," Josie said with a shrug.

I fished through my bag and grabbed my phone.

"Who are you calling?" Josie said.

"Detective Renfro."

"Most people would probably just walk down the stairs," Josie said.

"Oh, that's right," I said, frowning. "He's already here." But the call connected before I could hang up. "Hey, it's me…Yes, I know you're in the house. Head up to the rooftop terrace. We need to show you something." I ended the call and slipped the phone back into my bag. "He'll be right up."

Chapter 15

By the time Detective Renfro reached the rooftop, we were sitting at a table trying to make some sense of what we'd just seen. He sat down and couldn't miss our confused expressions.

"If I believed in ghosts, I'd probably be asking if you'd seen one. What's going on?"

Gerald gave him the short version, and the detective remained silent, occasionally jotting down a note. When Gerald finished, we focused on Detective Renfro and waited for his response.

"And you're sure it was the same dog?" he said eventually.

"Positive," I said, then glanced at Josie who nodded her agreement.

"Odd," the detective said, tapping the table with his pen. Then he caught the look I was giving him. "What is it?"

"Aren't you going to call to find out whose boat it is?" I said.

"I am," Detective Renfro said, jotting down another note before realizing I was still staring at him. "Oh, you mean, right now?"

"Well, it's really not for me to tell you how to do your job, Detective," I said.

"Geez, I must have missed that," he deadpanned.

Josie snorted loudly.

"Shut it."

"Your mother is right," the detective said, making the call. "You definitely have some pitbull in you."

We listened to his side of the short conversation then he put the phone on speaker and set it down on the table.

"They put me on hold while they take a look," he said, glancing around the rooftop. "Beautiful spot up here. You've done well, Gerald."

"Thanks," Gerald said, obviously preoccupied with other thoughts.

"Are you still there, Detective?" said a voice through the phone.

Detective Renfro took the phone off speaker and held it to his ear. Then he frowned as he stared out to sea.

"Okay, thanks, Mary," he said, then ended the call. "The boat is registered to William Quiver."

"Who the hell would steal a dead guy's boat?" Gerald said.

"And his dog," Josie said.

"Yeah, and his dog," Gerald said, nodding.

"My first guess would be whoever killed him," I said.

"Are you back on that again, Suzy?" Detective Renfro said. "That case is closed. Suicide as the official cause of death, remember?"

"I remember," I said, rubbing my forehead. "I'm just not buying it." I glanced back and forth at Gerald and Josie. "Did either one of you get a good look at the person driving the boat?"

"No, all I could see was his back," Gerald said.

"Me too," Josie said.

I exhaled loudly, baffled.

"Has the boat been reported as stolen?" I said.

"No," Detective Renfro said. "Maybe he gave the boat to somebody. He obviously wasn't going to need it. Along with instructions to take good care of his dog."

"If that was the case, why would he mention the dog in the note?" I said, my neurons slowly starting to fire.

"I don't know," the detective said with a shrug. "Maybe an additional insurance policy of some sort. You know, he was doing everything he could to make sure the dog ended up in good hands."

"Sounds thin," I said. "Are you going to send some people out to look for the boat?"

"Why would I do that?" the detective said.

"I can't believe you would ask such a dumb question," I said, my voice rising.

"Suzy," Josie said, placing a hand on my forearm. "Easy."

"No, it's quite all right, Josie," Detective Renfro said, sitting back in his chair and fixing a stare on me. "I'd like to hear what she's got on her mind."

"Careful what you wish for, Detective," Josie said, then patted my hand to get my attention. "Play nice."

"I'm fine," I said, then took a few moments to organize my thoughts. "Well, first of all, we have to look at Samantha's murder and Little Billy's…death as connected events."

"We do?" Detective Renfro said, raising an eyebrow.

"Isn't that what you've been thinking?" I said, surprised.

"Not for a second. Suzy, we've got a suicide on the beach, and a medical officer who was tragically murdered. Tell me. How on earth are they connected?"

It was a good question, and for the moment, I was stumped.

"Well, she was the one who examined Quiver's body," I said. Even to me, it sounded lame.

"She's was the frigging medical officer," the detective said. "Who else was gonna do it?"

"Yeah…but still," I said, firing blanks. "I still think you should try to find the boat."

"And do what?" Detective Renfro said. "Grill them about how they got their hands on the boat?"

"And the dog," Josie said.

"That would be a good start," I said, shrugging.

"Suzy, I know how you get sometimes. And your reputation is sterling. But at the moment, I'm dealing with an actual murder. And in case you haven't noticed," he said, glancing at Gerald. "I have a lot of eyes on me given the rather delicate political ramifications that go along with it. With all due respect, Premier."

"Point taken," Gerald said softly. Then he shook his head. "I'm afraid I don't see a connection either."

"Oh, there's definitely a connection," I said, staring off into the distance.

"Have you found what you're looking for, Detective?" Gerald said.

"No, sir. And off the record, I seriously doubt if we will. There's no way you killed Samantha."

"Thank you, Detective," Gerald said. "I appreciate that."

I was dying to have the conversation about possible links between the fifty million Quiver had been looking for and Samantha's death, but I bit my tongue. Moments later, two heads appeared at the top of the stairs, and both uniformed cops were soon heading our way.

"You guys ready to go?" Detective Renfro said, getting to his feet.

"Not quite, Detective," Officer Givens said, then held up a sealed evidence bag for us to see. "Nine-millimeter."

"What?" Gerald said, his eyes going wide.

"Is this your gun, sir?" Officer Givens said.

"I've never seen it before," Gerald said. "I hate guns. And refuse to have one in the house."

"Ah, crap," Josie whispered.

"Yeah," I whispered back. "Not good."

Detective Renfro examined the bag then handed it to other the cop before turning around to face Gerald.

"I'm sorry, sir. But I'm afraid you're going to have to come with us."

"Yeah, I get it," Gerald said, getting up from the table.

Officer Givens reached for his handcuffs and started to head for the table. He stopped when Detective Renfro grabbed his elbow.

"Those won't be necessary," the detective said, shaking his head at the uniformed cop.

"But policy dictates-"

"No, absolutely not," Detective Renfro said, shaking his head. "Show some respect."

"Man, you can't catch a break, can you?" I said to Officer Givens.

"What?" the cop said.

"You're just dying to use those things."

"I could use them on you," he said, giving me his best cop glare.

"Do it, and you'll be breathing through a tube," Josie said.

"I beg your pardon?" Officer Given said, focusing his laser-stare on her.

"You heard me."

"I don't see where this is any of your business."

"Anybody who even thinks about putting their hands on her is always my business," Josie growled.

"Aren't you sweet?" I said, beaming at her.

"I got your back, Sister."

Officer Givens struck his most menacing pose, which I had to admit wasn't bad, then flashed me an evil grin.

"Ms. Chandler, we're not dealing with a bunch of stolen roosters here," the cop said.

I flinched when he referenced the time Josie and I had been arrested for stealing some roosters while trying to bust up an illegal cockfighting ring operating on the island. The situation had been embarrassing for everyone involved, and we'd almost ended up getting deported.

"Ancient history," I said, quickly recovering. "And it has nothing to do with this situation."

"I merely point it out to highlight how you have a tendency to end up in the middle of things that are absolutely no business of yours," Officer Givens said, then glanced at Josie. "Or any of your concern, either."

"I guess we're going to disagree about that, Officer Givens," I snapped.

"Yeah," Josie said. "Somebody is trying to set Gerald up. You can bet we're going to get involved."

"Exactly," I said, nodding at her. "Try and stop us."

"I'm within my rights to charge both of you with obstruction."

"Stuff a sock in it," I said, laughing at the cop.

"Yeah, blow it out your-"

"Enough," Detective Renfro snapped. "Put the handcuffs away, Givens. And you two, please sit down and do your best to keep your mouths shut."

"Well, since you asked nicely," I said, sitting down and folding my arms across my chest.

"I'm going to be charged with her murder, aren't I?" Gerald said to the detective.

"I'm afraid that's a distinct possibility, sir. Especially if we get a match on the gun."

"Oh, it'll definitely match," I said to one in particular.

"Do you have something you'd like to tell us?" Officer Givens said.

"I'm not talking to you," I said. "Gerald, we'll call your lawyer and organize bail as soon as we can."

"Thanks, Suzy," Gerald said. "Oh, you might want to also call Marjorie and have her clear my calendar for the next several days."

"You got it. Hang in there. We'll get this all sorted out soon."

"I hope you're right, Suzy," Gerald said, then headed for the stairs followed closely by the two uniformed officers.

"Hang on," I called out.

Officer Givens came to a stop and wheeled around.

"What is it now?"

"Where did you find the gun?"

"In his golf bag," the cop said, then headed down the stairs and disappeared from sight.

Soon, Josie and I were alone on the rooftop.

"This is bad," I said after a long silence.

"Yeah. The worst."

"That pretty much sums it up."

"And you're sure this is somehow linked with Quiver's death?"

"I'm positive."

"Really?" she said, obviously having a hard time believing it.

"Yup."

"You got any ideas about how to prove it?"

"Nope."

"Well, I'm sure you'll come up with a strategy soon."

"Maybe," I said, getting to my feet. "But first things, first. Let's go see what we can do about bailing out the Premier."

"The press is going to have a field day," Josie said. "Not to mention being camped out in front of his house."

"Yeah. I was just thinking we should pack a bag."

"You planning on taking a trip?"

"No, but Gerald is."

"And where exactly is he going?" she said, frowning at me.

"Our place. We've got tons of room."

"I like it," Josie said, gently punching me on the shoulder. "You're a good friend, Suzy."

"Thanks," I said, heading for the stairs. "But right now, what I really need to be is a good snoop."

Chapter 16

Word traveled fast, and by the time we arrived at the police station, several members of the media were camped outside, and the lobby was overflowing with cops, politicians and several of Gerald's friends and associates. We found my mother and Paulie sitting on a bench inside, and when they spotted us, they both got to their feet. My mother nodded for us to follow, and she led the way into a quiet alcove away from prying eyes and ears.

"You got here fast," I said.

"Your message sounded urgent," she said. "Albeit a bit cryptic."

"I didn't want to go into a lot of detail over the phone."

"Nobody is talking," my mother said. "What's going on?"

"They found the murder weapon at Gerald's house," I said.

"Ah, damn," my mother whispered. "Of all the crap he's gotten away with, now he's going to go down for something he didn't do?"

"Gotten away with? Care to elaborate, Mom?" I said, frowning.

"Figure of speech, darling."

"Well, let's stay focused on what we do know," Paulie said. "The first is we know he's innocent."

"Absolutely," my mother said, nodding.

"The second is we need to figure out who did kill her in a hurry," Paulie said.

All of them focused on me, and I eventually scowled back at them.

"Hey, you mind giving me a bit of time?" I said. "Geez, I haven't even had lunch yet."

"Get your mind off food, darling."

"It's a figure of speech, Mom. My point is I'm going to need some time to sort this mess out."

"Don't take too long," my mother said.

"Yeah, people love a juicy political scandal," Josie said. "This one's going to go viral in a hurry. And it's a total career killer."

"Forget about his career, dear," my mother said. "We need to focus on keeping him out of prison."

"What do we know?" Paulie said, vigorously scratching the back of his head.

"Fleas?" Josie deadpanned.

"Funny," Paulie said. "No, sunburn. I went fishing the other day and forgot my hat. It itches like crazy."

"I hate when that happens," I said, staring off at the far wall. "We know that Little Billy was probably down here looking for his old man's fifty million."

"And had Gerald in his sights," Paulie said, nodding.

"Yes," I said. "And for some reason, somebody needed to remove Quiver from the equation."

"But who and why?" Paulie said.

"I have no idea," I said, rubbing my forehead. "But it has to be tied to the money, right?"

"It usually is," Paulie said. "But don't underestimate the power of revenge."

"Hey, I lived with her for years," I said with a grin as I nodded at my mother. "I'm very familiar with the revenge play."

"You're a real hoot, darling. Now, if you've got it all out of your system, would it be possible for you to focus on the matter at hand?"

"Quiver had to be working with a partner," I said eventually. "That's the only thing that makes sense."

"The dog," Josie said, glancing at me.

"Yeah," I said with a nod.

My mother and Paulie gave both us blank stares.

"We saw the Weimaraner on a boat while we were at Gerald's place," I said.

"And?" my mother said, confused.

"And Ruby was on a boat called Wanderlust. Detective Renfro tracked it down. It was Little Billy's boat."

"How on earth did you see it?" Paulie said.

"Gerald has a telescope on his rooftop terrace," Josie said. "He said he uses it to look at the stars."

My mother snorted.

"Among other things," she said, laughing.

"You think Little Billy's partner was the one on the boat?" Paulie said.

"It had to be, right?" I said. "But since the cops refuse to budge off their suicide theory and won't even try to find the boat, I guess we'll never know."

"Little Billy didn't kill himself," Paulie said. "But his partner taking him out. I have no trouble making that work. It happens all the time. What do you think?"

"I keep going back to the fifty million," I said. "I think Little Billy somehow found out about the missing money, came down here to get it, then learned it was gone. And the only lead he had about where it might be was Gerald. So, he decided to put the squeeze on him."

"But got killed before he could get very far," Paulie said.

"Or do any real damage to Gerald," I said, nodding.

Josie cleared her throat. All three of us turned toward her.

"You got popcorn stuck in your throat, or do you have something to say?" I said.

"I was thinking, while Gerald had absolutely no motive to kill Samantha, he had more than enough to do something about Quiver."

"No," I said, shaking my head. "He didn't do that, either."

"How can you be so sure, Suzy?" she said.

"Because we're talking about Gerald," I said firmly.

"I know," Josie said. "And I love the guy. But we need to look at the facts. Quiver was a real threat to him. And we all know how much Gerald loves being the guy in charge down here."

"No," my mother said. "I agree with you about how much he loves his job, but Gerald's too much of a pragmatist to take a risk like that. And he's way too much of a coward. No, there's no way. Not a chance."

"Maybe he had somebody else do it," Josie said. "You know, he hired someone to take Quiver out."

"No," my mother said, shaking her head. "Way too risky. And Gerald might have had to divulge some things he needs to keep to himself."

"Like helping himself to something that didn't belong to him?" I said.

"Please keep your voice down, darling. We are standing in the middle of the police station."

I nodded and reached for my phone.

"Who are you calling?" my mother said.

"Chef Claire. She's watching Max, and I need to let her know we might be a bit late getting home." I glanced around the crowded lobby as I waited for the call to connect. "I wonder what tomorrow's headline is going to be?"

"Premier charged with murder would be my first guess," Josie said.

"Hey," I said into the phone. "How's it going? No, let her sleep...Look, there's a bit of an issue we need to deal with...Oh, you heard. News travels fast...Yeah, they found it in his golf bag…You're taking the night off, right? We might be here for a while. You mind feeding Max when she wakes up? There are several bottles of milk in the fridge…Thanks, Chef Claire. Yeah, we'll let you know as soon as we hear anything. Oh, Gerald's probably going to be staying with us for at least a few days until the dust settles…Cool. Thanks, Chef Claire."

I put my phone away then caught the look my mother was giving me.

"What?" I said, frowning.

"What was that about Gerald staying with you?"

"We thought it would be a good idea if he didn't go back to his house. The press is going to be camped out there."

"Good idea," my mother said.

"And I thought our place would be better than yours," I said. "Everyone on the island knows how close you two are, and your house would be the next place the press would look. And I know how you hate uninvited guests."

"Especially of the media variety," my mother said, nodding. "Good call, darling. That's very sweet of you."

"It's Gerald," I said with a shrug. "Now, our next challenge is to get him out of here without anybody knowing where he's going. That's the problem."

"What problem are you talking about?" Detective Renfro said as he approached from the back end of the police station where the interview rooms were located.

"Hey, Detective," I said. "We were just talking about a way to get Gerald out of here without the press knowing where he's going."

"Okay. At the moment, he's not going anywhere. But I'll play. Where is he going after he makes bail?"

"He's gonna be staying at our place," I said. "But don't tell anybody."

"Probably not a bad strategy," he said. "You're going to need a diversion to throw thc jackals off thc trail."

"Can you help us out with that?" my mother said.

He gave it some thought, then nodded.

"Yeah, I think I can. And it certainly won't be the first time I've had to do it," Detective Renfro said. "You guys sticking around?"

"We are," my mother said.

"Okay, I'll find you after he makes bail. We'll figure something out."

"Thank you, Detective," my mother said.

"And Gerald's lawyer mentioned you'll be covering his bail."

"I have my checkbook right here," she said, patting her purse.

"It's good to have rich friends, huh?" he said with a grin. "Okay, I need to get back in there."

"Any update?" I said.

"Nope," he said, shaking his head. "Gerald's adamant he never met the woman, doesn't own a gun, and hasn't got a clue about how it got in his golf bag."

"And you still believe him, right?" I said.

"I do," Detective Renfro said. "But what I believe won't make a whit of difference in a courtroom."

"This is never going to trial," I said, shaking my head.

"You know something I don't, Suzy?"

"Not yet," I said, beaming at him.

"Okay," he said, laughing. "I'll see you guys later. And there's some really crappy coffee down the hall if you need it at some point."

"Thanks, Detective," my mother said. "Any idea how much longer this is going to take?"

"My best guess is a couple of hours at least," he said, then waved as he headed down the hall and entered one of the interview rooms.

"Well, the last thing I want is crappy coffee," my mother said.

"Why don't I do a quick food run?" Josie said.

"You're an angel," I said, my stomach rumbling at the thought of food.

Josie jotted down our orders then I tossed her the keys to the SUV. After she left, the three of us sat down and spent the next few minutes in silence glancing around the alcove. Several individuals we recognized walked past and gave us small waves as they went about their business.

"Penny for your thoughts, darling."

"I was just wondering if one of Gerald's rivals, or even someone in his cabinet, might be the one behind this."

"I suppose anything's possible," she said, checking her phone for messages.

"This all has to be connected," Paulie said. "You know, with what happened to Little Billy."

"I tried to tell the cops that, but they didn't buy it," I said. "Great minds think alike, huh?"

"Geez, don't even say that, darling," my mother, not looking up from her phone. "You're more than enough to deal with. The last thing I need is the two of you thinking the same way."

"Watch and learn, Mom. Just watch and learn."

"Just figure out what the hell is going on, darling. That will be more than enough to make me happy."

"So, what's next?" Paulie said.

"I think it's time we tracked down the bank president," I said.

"The one who worked with Gerald on getting their hands on the fifty million?" Paulie said.

"Yeah," I said. "I don't know if it's going to be worth the effort. But it's definitely a missing piece of the puzzle."

"You got any ideas about how to find him?" Paulie said.

"I've got one."

Chapter 17

The diversion Detective Renfro came up with worked to perfection. When Gerald finally posted bail, the cops made a big show of pulling three black government SUVs directly in front of the police station. They sat there for a few minutes before slowing making their way down the driveway that led to the back entrance. My mother and Paulie remained in front of the station in her car, then pulled in behind the three government SUVs when they exited the station about ten minutes later. Soon, a small caravan of vehicles loaded with members of the media was following in hot pursuit.

I had called Josie while she was on her food run and asked her to park in the back. As such, when we pulled out with Josie in the passenger seat and Gerald sprawled out on the floor behind her with a blanket over him, not a single person still in front of the station noticed. We headed straight for home, and I parked in the garage. Gerald climbed out of the SUV and immediately went to work putting his hair back in place.

"Were you comfy back there?" Josie said.

"Not as comfy as I would have been with you," he said, grinning at her. "We could have snuggled."

"Sorry, Gerald," she deadpanned. "I've never had a thing for criminals."

"Ouch," he said, feigning hurt feelings. "So, what are the sleeping arrangements? I assume I'll be bunking with you, right?"

"Sure," Josie said. "As long as you can get past Captain without losing an arm. He can be a bit rough on uninvited guests."

"Thanks for the warning," he said, then turned serious and glanced back and forth at us. "I appreciate you guys doing this."

"No problem, Gerald," I said, opening the back hatch and handing him the bag we'd packed. "You can stay as long as you need to. C'mon, let's get you settled in, and then we'll head to the pool for a sundowner."

"Perfect," he said. "Alcohol will definitely be the highlight of my day."

"The guest room is the third one on the right," I said. "Go on ahead. Josie and I need to do a few things with the dogs."

We watched him head off then Josie frowned at me.

"What was all that?" she said, draping her bag over her shoulder.

"What?"

"The guy gets arrested for murder, and the first thing he does is turn into a major flirt?"

"Yeah, I noticed," I said, staring after the Premier who had stopped midway across the lawn to say hello to the house dogs. "His manliness probably feels threatened. I'm sure it's just a defense mechanism. Did it bother you?"

"No, of course not," she said, laughing. "I can handle Gerald. It was just out of character for him. It surprised me."

"It must be a day for them, huh?" I said, reaching for my phone.

"It's definitely having its moments. Who are you calling?"

"Our friend in Washington."

"I'm going to say hi to the dogs," Josie said. "Say hello to Agent Tompkins for me."

I nodded and placed the call. I sat down on a large storage trunk in the corner of the garage and waited for the agent to answer.

"This is Tompkins."

"Hey, it's me."

"Suzy. I guess it's time to put you on speed dial. What's up?"

"I was wondering if you've heard the news."

"All I hear is news, Suzy. And most of it bad. What are you referring to?"

"Geez, I would have thought it would be on the FBI's radar by now," I said, frowning.

"I just got out of a three-hour meeting," he said. "And I haven't been near a computer or my phone. What's up?"

"Gerald was arrested for murder earlier today," I said.

"Wow," Agent Tompkins whispered. "So, the cops figured out a way to tie him to Quiver's murder?"

"No, that's still being listed as a suicide."

"Somebody else died, huh?" he said. "And don't tell me nothing gets past me, okay?"

"The thought never crossed my mind."

"Well, don't keep me in suspense," Agent Tompkins said, the sound of him tapping a pen on his desk coming in loud and clear through the phone.

"That's an annoying habit, Agent Tompkins."

"Sorry. Who died?"

"A woman by the name of Samantha Powers. She was a relief medical officer covering for someone while he was on vacation," I said.

"Medical officer? She didn't happen to be the one who handled Quiver's body by any chance, was she?"

"She was," I said softly.

"Interesting. And they charged Gerald with her murder?" Agent Tompkins said. "Let me guess, a lover's quarrel. Gerald's got quite the reputation as a womanizer."

"Sure, he dates a lot," I said, feeling the need to defend the Premier. "But I'm not sure I'd call him a womanizer."

"Tomato, tomahto," Agent Tompkins said dismissively.

"But Gerald swears he'd never even met her," I said.

"And you believe him?"

"I do."

"Okay, that's good enough for me," Agent Tompkins said. "What happened to her?"

"One in the back of the head. Nine-millimeter."

"That'll do the trick," the FBI agent said. "How did they tie it to Gerald?"

"They found her body in the trunk of his car," I said. "And today the cops found the murder weapon at his house. It was in his golf bag."

Agent Tompkins whistled softly into the phone.

"Have the cops matched the gun?"

"No, but I'll be very surprised if they don't," I said.

"Geez, what the hell was the guy thinking?"

"He didn't do it," I snapped.

"Incriminating evidence notwithstanding, right?"

"He's being set up."

"Well, if he is, whoever's doing it has done a great job," Agent Tompkins said. "Okay, I get it. You want some help clearing Gerald. What can I do for you?"

"Robert Bentley."

"William Mercedes," Agent Tompkins deadpanned.

"What?"

"I thought we were playing some sort of name the car game," he said, laughing. "Who the heck is Robert Bentley?"

"He was a local bank president when Slash Quiver's fifty-million went missing," I said.

"And you think there's a connection between Quiver's death and the medical officer's murder?"

"I do. Unfortunately, I haven't been able to convince the local cops there is."

"That makes sense," he said. "They'd have to admit they were wrong about how Little Billy died. And cops hate admitting when they've made a mistake. Especially to someone like you."

"Someone like me?" I said, my voice rising.

"A civilian," he said. "Relax, Suzy. How many times do I have to tell you not to take this stuff personally?"

"Yeah, I really need to start working on that," I said, rubbing my forehead. "Anyway, I was just wondering if you guys have a file on Robert Bentley."

"Is he a U.S. citizen?"

"I have no idea," I said. "But let's start with that assumption."

"Okay," he said, after a long silence. "I guess I can do that much. If you're convinced Gerald's innocent."

"I am," I said.

"According to the notes I see here, Gerald's been very cooperative with us when we needed help," Agent Tompkins said. "Let me take a look and see what we come up with."

I listened to the sound of his keyboard clacking, which was followed by another lengthy silence.

"Are you still there, Agent Tompkins?"

"I am. I'm a slow reader."

"So, you do have a file on him?"

"Oh, yeah," the agent said. "At least we did."

I frowned at his comment but remained silent.

"We closed the file recently."

"You cleared him?" I said.

"Not exactly. In fact, from what I'm seeing, we were closing in on him at the time."

"Let me guess, he's dead," I said.

"Your batting average continues to be outstanding."

"What happened to him?"

"Hang on," he said. "I haven't read that far yet." He fell silent, then softly whistled again. "Son of a gun. What do you know?"

"Please don't tell me he got one in the back of the head," I said, squeezing the phone tight.

"If I didn't tell you that, I'd be holding information back from you," he said. "I can't believe it."

"Nine-millimeter?"

"Yup."

"Do you have the ballistics?" I said, then prepared myself for his answer.

"I'm sure they're around somewhere," he said. "Since Bentley was on our radar, we officially took charge of the case from the local cops."

"Did you find the murder weapon?"

"Nope."

"Where's the bullet at the moment?" I said, again rubbing my forehead.

I waited out another extended silence and did my best to remain patient.

"Looks like our Bridgetown field office," he said.

"Bridgetown? Barbados?" I said, surprised.

"Yeah, we have an office down there that handles the Caribbean," Agent Tompkins said.

"Was that where he was killed?" I said.

"Yup. He got shot on his sailboat that was anchored offshore."

"When was this?"

"About six months ago," he said.

"What was he doing that caught the FBI's attention?"

"I don't think that's really relevant, Suzy."

"Not relevant because it's classified?" I said, tossing my line into the water.

"Not relevant because it's none of your frigging business."

"There's no need to get snarky, Agent Tompkins."

"Whatever Bentley was up to in the islands has nothing to do with Gerald or his current situation."

"You're positive?"

"Trust me on this one," he said. "There is no way Gerald was involved in what Bentley was doing."

"I suppose that makes me feel a bit better," I said, my mind racing a thousand miles an hour.

"Hang on. But this situation does raise an interesting question," Agent Tompkins said. "You said on a previous call that Gerald and a bank president worked together on their Slash Quiver problem."

"I did?" I said, trying to deflect. "Are you sure?"

"Nice try," he said, laughing. "Let me ask you a question."

"Well, that's kinda my job," I said, laughing along with him. "But go right ahead."

"Has Gerald been to Barbados in the past year?"

"I have no idea."

"But you can find out, right?"

"I suppose I could," I said, immediately on guard. "What are you implying, Agent Tompkins?"

"I'm not implying anything. I'm just asking."

"Is that your way of telling me you never caught the guy who shot Bentley?"

"Well done, Suzy. You're really on your game today," he said. "No, Bentley's shooter is listed in the report as an unidentified assailant."

"And you think Gerald might be the guy?" I said.

"I'm not thinking anything. I merely asked if the guy had been to Barbados," Agent Tompkins said.

"And if he has?"

"Let's just say it would be an interesting coincidence. Especially if he happened to be there when Bentley was killed."

I fell silent as I pondered the implications of what I'd just been told.

"Let me ask you something else," Agent Tompkins said.

"What's that?"

"How well do you know the Premier?"

"Very well. He's one of our best friends down here."

"Are you going to be seeing him soon?'

"Yeah, I like my chances," I said.

"Well, do yourself a favor and keep your eyes and ears open. There's a lot of people walking around carrying some very dark secrets."

"Gerald? A threat? Not a chance."

"He's never lied to you, or maybe kept something from you?"

I thought about the missing fifty million. Then I shook my head at the possibility recent events had been provoked by Gerald's concern his decision to keep some of the money might leak.

"Are you still there?" he said.

"Yeah. I'm here."

"Look, all I'm saying is to stay on your toes."

"I'll sleep with one eye open."

"What?"

"Nothing," I said. "I'll let you go. Thanks for your help, Agent Tompkins."

"No problem. I do love a good murder mystery. Call me if you need help, or if something breaks open down there."

"Will do," I said. "Oh, Josie says hi."

"Right back at her. Give my best to everyone. And keep your head down, Suzy. This whole thing sounds pretty bizarre."

"That's the word for it."

Chapter 18

We ate dinner outside near the pool, a pleasant but subdued couple of hours given the gravity of Gerald's situation. But it didn't seem to affect our appetites, and we all ate heartily and made it a point not to discuss the day's events or ponder out loud what the future might hold for our good friend.

Paulie and Josie's eyes both landed on the remaining swordfish steak at the same time.

"You plan on eating that last piece of fish?" Paulie said.

"Trick question?" Josie deadpanned.

"I'll split it with you," he said.

"Deal," Josie said, expertly slicing the fish in half before placing the pieces on their plates. "Outstanding job, Chef Claire."

"Thanks," Chef Claire said, swirling the wine in her glass as she stared off into the distance. "Can I ask you something, Gerald?"

"Asking permission," he said, glancing at me. "What a nice change."

"Shut it," I said, stifling a laugh.

"Of course, Chef Claire," Gerald said, sitting back in his chair and giving her his undivided attention.

"This is going to sound blunt, so I apologize upfront," she said. "But if someone wants you taken out that badly, why bother going to these lengths to set you up? Why not just shoot you and get it over with?"

"Well, she's right," Josie said, pausing mid-bite. "That was blunt."

"No, I'm serious," Chef Claire said. "It's a clever plan, but I can think of a dozen ways it could have fallen apart before it ever got off the ground."

"Captain," Josie said, her voice rising. "You know better. And you've had your dinner. No begging at the table. Now, go play."

Captain woofed his displeasure and trotted off toward the edge of the pool where the other house dogs were occupying different lounge chairs. I watched the Newfie as he climbed up on an empty lounger and flashed Josie a final dirty look before settling in and draping his head across his front paws.

"You hurt his feelings," my mother said with a laugh then stroked Queen, her King Charles spaniel, who was occupying her usual spot perched on her lap. "Didn't she, Queen?"

"He'll get over it," Josie said. "And that reminds me, I need to take him to the shelter in the morning."

"What for?" I said.

"He needs a booster shot, and I want to trim his nails," Josie said, smiling at the Newfie who continued to pout. "If you think he's grumpy now, just wait until he gets there. He hates having his nails done."

"Just do it here," I said. "I'll give you a hand."

"No, I don't have what I need for his shot. Besides, I told Teresa I'd stop by and take a look at a new litter of puppies."

"I think I'll tag along," I said. "I need to take care of a few things over there as well."

"Good luck getting him out of the passenger seat," Josie said, nodding at the Newfie. "He loves riding shotgun."

Chef Claire sat quietly, waiting patiently for us to finish our conversation then she focused on Gerald.

"To answer your question, Chcf Claire," Gerald said. "I don't have a clue."

"There has to be a common thread running through this," she said, then glanced at me.

"What?" I said, staring back at her.

"That's your cue," she said.

Everyone at the table laughed.

"I do have a few thoughts on the matter," I said.

"Here we go," Josie said, refilling everyone's wine glass. "Okay, Snoopmeister. Enlighten us."

"Well, I'm pretty far from enlightenment," I said, trying to sort through the jumbled mess of thoughts and questions that had been running wild since my earlier conversation with Agent Tompkins. I'd been holding off having the conversation throughout dinner, but this seemed like as good a time as any. "The common thread is obviously Little Billy Quiver. There has to be some sort of link."

"Even though he's dead, darling?"

"Especially since he's dead," I said, rubbing my forehead. Then I remembered the promise I'd made to Gerald and my mother about keeping my mouth shut. I made solid eye contact with the Premier. "Before I go on, there are a couple people at the table who don't know all the details, Gerald."

"What details?" Josie said, immediately on point.

"Yeah, spill," Chef Claire said.

"In case you weren't clear about who I was referring to," I said, gesturing at my two best friends.

"You haven't told them?" my mother said, surprised. "Well done, darling."

"I told you I could keep a secret," I said, then refocused on Gerald.

"What are you talking about?" Josie said.

"Hang on," I said, holding up a hand. "Hold your horses."

Gerald gave it some serious thought, then nodded.

"Go ahead," he said. "It's probably all going to come out anyway."

"This sounds juicy," Jose said to Chef Claire.

"Yeah, somebody's been holding out on us," she said.

"I'm sorry, guys," I said. "You'll know in a minute why I couldn't say anything."

"Are you sure about this, Gerald?" my mother said.

"Hey, I'm among friends, right?" he said with a shrug. He motioned to me that I had the floor.

"About twenty years ago," I said, starting slowly. "Back when Gerald was still a lawyer working on behalf of...let's call them some of the shadier characters who like to hide their money down here, he came across fifty million dollars. Fifty million made from an illegal activity that bothered him a great deal."

"Such as?" Josie said.

"Heroin," I said.

"Score a point for Gerald," Chef Claire said, raising her glass to him in salute. "And you turned the guy in, right?"

"Not exactly," Gerald said.

"Oh, I don't think I'm gonna like where this is going," Josie said.

"Gerald worked with the president of the bank where the account was located, and they came up with a way to...let's say, move the money somewhere it could do the most good," I said.

"Okay," Josie said, her eyes narrowing. "What did you do with it?"

"We built a hospital with it," Gerald said.

"You did?" Chef Claire said. "A very noble gesture."

"Thanks," Gerald said. "We felt good about it at the time."

"Which hospital?" Josie said.

"The one near my office."

"Nice," Josie said. "They provide a lot of services to women and kids, right?"

"They do," Gerald said, glancing at my mother who was slowly shaking her head at him.

I caught their silent exchange and knew from experience that my mother wanted her own anonymous gift kept quiet. I beamed at her as a swell of pride emerged. She insisted on preserving her anonymity and never talked about the wide range of philanthropic activities she was involved with.

"That was a wonderful thing to do, Gerald," Chef Claire said. "You're interactions with a major heroin dealer notwithstanding."

"I didn't know how he made his money," Gerald said. "At first."

"And when you found out you decided to take his fifty million?" Josie said.

"Pretty much," Gerald said, then took a sip of wine. Then he shrugged it off. "After a fashion."

"Uh-oh," Josie said to Chef Claire. "I think the story is about to take a turn for the worse."

"Yeah," Chef Claire said, studying Gerald's expression. "Whose fifty million was it?"

Gerald glanced at me, but I shook my head and gestured it was his story to tell. He nodded and glanced back and forth at Josie and Chef Claire.

"Slash Quiver," he said softly.

"Little Billy's old man?" Chef Claire said.

"The very one," Gerald said.

"And he came down here looking for it?" Chef Claire said.

"That appears to be the case," he said.

"Why on earth would he wait twenty years to come after his dad's money?" Chef Claire said.

"My best guess is he didn't know he had it. Or didn't know where his old man kept it," Gerald said.

"He spent twenty years looking for it?" Josie said, stunned.

"It was fifty million bucks, dear," my mother said. "How long would you keep looking for it?"

"Until the end of time," Josie said, then exhaled loudly.

"Hang on," Chef Claire said. "With all due respect, Gerald, you're a politician. If you donated fifty million to build a hospital, why the hell isn't your name on it?"

"We wanted it to be anonymous," Gerald whispered.

"Yeah," Chef Claire said, raising an eyebrow at him. "And my dream is to play third base for the Yankees."

"You're starting to think more like her every day," Josie said, nodding in my direction.

"I guess it rubs off over time, huh?" Chef Claire said, laughing. "C'mon, Gerald. Spill your guts."

"We may have decided to keep some of the money," he said after a lengthy silence.

"There it is," Chef Claire said. "Geez, Gerald. What on earth were you thinking?"

"Obviously, that he could get away with it," Josie said, then turned to the Premier. "How much did you keep?"

"Only a couple million," he said with a shrug. "And I had to split it."

"With the bank president, right?" Chef Claire said.

"Yeah."

"Is he still around?" Chef Claire said.

"No, he's long gone," Gerald said, reaching for the wine bottle to refill his glass.

"You got that right," I blurted.

The tone of my voice caught everyone's attention, and they all stared at me.

"What?" Gerald said.

"I said you got that right," I said.

The premier remained focused on me. Eventually, I leaned forward and placed both elbows on the table.

"I've been waiting to talk with you alone about it," I said. "But since you've pretty much laid it all out, I guess it can't hurt."

"There's more?" Josie said.

"Oh, yeah. There's more."

"Well, I can't wait to hear it," Paulie said. "Because I am baffled why we suddenly have two dead people on our hands and Gerald is being set up for killing one of them."

"Three," I said.

"Three?" Gerald whispered.

"Yeah." I paused to take a sip of wine and collect my thoughts. Then I continued. "Have you done much traveling lately, Gerald?"

"What on earth does that have to do with the price of fish, darling?"

"Hang on, Mom. It'll make sense soon."

"Have I done much traveling?" Gerald said. "That's kind of a question out of left field, Suzy."

"It is," I said. "Have you?"

"Traveling? Not really," he said. "And only for business when I have."

"Where have you been?"

"What's going on, Suzy? Have the cops deputized you or something? You want to put me on the grill and force me to talk? Maybe a little waterboarding in the pool?"

"Don't be so dramatic, Gerald," I said.

"I'm sorry, but in case you haven't noticed, I've had quite a day."

"Well, prepare yourself," I said. "Because there's a chance it's about to get a whole lot worse."

"I can hardly see where that's possible, darling."

I ignored my mother's comment.

"Where have you traveled recently, Gerald?" I said.

"Well, let's see," he said, giving it some thought. "About a year ago, I was in New York for a few days dealing with some money guys. On the way back, I spent a few days in Miami catching up with friends. And the only other time I've been off-island was to give a speech at a conference."

"In Barbados, right?" I said.

Gerald's eyes went wide, which I hoped was caused by surprise rather than guilt.

"How the hell did you know that?"

"I spoke with Agent Tompkins earlier today."

"You called the FBI?" Gerald said, stunned. "Again?"

"Why on earth would you do that, darling?"

"Because you told me to, Mom."

"I most certainly did not."

"Maybe not in so many words," I said with a shrug. "But you basically ordered me to figure out who was trying to set Gerald up. Remember?"

"I do," my mother said. "But did you really need to involve the Feebs?"

"I decided it was time to see if I could get some information on Robert Bentley."

"Robert Bentley?" Josie said, looking over at Chef Claire. "The plot thickens, huh?"

"Who the heck is that?" Chef Claire said.

"Oh, I know," Josie said, raising a finger in the air. "He was the bank president you worked with to steal the fifty million, wasn't he?"

"Well played," I said, impressed.

"I have my moments," Josie said, then sat back and waited for me to continue.

"I couldn't get the thought that the fifty million was behind all this out of my head. So, I figured it was time to see if Bentley had somehow gotten on the FBI's radar. You know, since he had already stolen fifty million, maybe he decided to stay in the game after he left the islands."

"We didn't steal fifty million," Gerald snapped. "We donated it to charity."

"Settle down, Gerald," my mother said. "You'll get your day in court."

"What?" Gerald said, glaring at my mother.

"Figure of speech," she said, patting his hand. "Please continue, darling."

"Anyway, Agent Tompkins confirmed the FBI did have a file on Bentley," I said.

"A file? Oh, this is not good," Gerald said.

"No, that part is okay, Gerald. The file they had on him only dealt with things Bentley had been involved with after he left Cayman."

"What sort of things?" Gerald said.

"Agent Tompkins wouldn't share any details. But he was definitely in their sights."

"Did Agent Tompkins tell you where Bentley is?" Gerald said.

"He did." I took another sip of wine before continuing. "Barbados."

"Barbados?" Gerald said, his eyes wide. "And that's why you asked me about my travels?"

"Yup," I said. "You were there, right?"

"Yes, but only to give a speech at the conference. I had no idea he was there. I haven't seen or heard from him in twenty years. Did Agent Tompkins tell you anything about what he's been up to?"

"Not really," I said. "This was about six months ago, right?"

"It was. That's a blast from the past. Bentley was quite the character. I wonder what sort of mischief he's getting up to these days."

"Not much," I said with a frown. "In fact, you could say, he's gone…underground."

"Underground? As in hiding?" Paulie said.

"No," I whispered with a shake of my head.

"Dead?" Paulie said.

"Very much so."

"Oh, this can't be good news," Gerald said, rubbing his forehead. "What happened to him?"

"He got shot on his boat," I said.

"Did they catch his killer?" Gerald said. "Please tell me they caught his killer, Suzy."

"I wish I could. But they haven't. Yet."

"Are you insinuating something, Suzy?" the premier said, his voice again rising.

"No, I'm not, Gerald," I said. "It's just there are some clues that may end up pointing back to you."

"Like what?" Gerald said. "I never left the hotel the entire time I was down there."

"I believe you," I said. "But there are some similarities in the way he was killed."

"One in the back of the head?" Paulie said.

"Yeah. Nine-millimeter."

"Does the FBI have anything tangible?" Paulie said.

"No murder weapon," I said. "But they have ballistics."

"Oh, crap," my mother said. "Are you thinking the gun they found at Gerald's place might match that bullet?"

"I'll be very surprised if it doesn't, Mom," I said, my eyes beginning to well with tears. "Somebody is orchestrating a masterful plan. And if it didn't involve you, Gerald, I'd have to say I was incredibly impressed with how they've done it."

"But how is this possible?" Gerald said, his hand shaking as he reached for his wine glass.

"My best guess at the moment, but I think I'm right, Little Billy finally figured out where his old man had kept his money. And he managed to track down Bentley who was the bank president at the time. He confronted him on his boat, probably threatened him, or worse, and Bentley spilled his guts about what the two of you had done. Then he parked one in his head and left."

"And came here looking for Gerald," Paulie said. "That's definitely something Little Billy would have done."

"Fifty million," my mother said, shrugging. "Say no more."

"Yeah," Paulie said. "This is bad."

"The worst," Gerald said. "I'm so screwed."

"Double murder and felony grand theft?" Josie said, shaking her head. "You're way past screwed, Gerald."

"Thanks for the vote of confidence," Gerald said, making a face at her.

"I was just agreeing with you," Josie said, then gently punched him on the shoulder. "But try not to worry too much."

"Why on earth not?" Gerald said.

"Because the Snoopmeister is going to figure out exactly what is going on," she said. "Aren't you?"

Before I could respond, I heard the unmistakable sound of the gate fronting the beach click open. Even in the dim evening light, the trademark Panama hat the intruder was wearing was immediately recognizable. Upwind from us, it was clear the man didn't hear the low, threatening growls all four house dogs were emitting. He closed the gate behind him and began to slowly make his way across the lawn toward us.

"We've got company," I said, nodding in his general direction.

"We'll just see about that," my mother said, starting to get to her feet.

"No, hang on, Mrs. C.," Josie said. "Let's wait a sec until he gets a bit closer to the pool. And everyone should act like we don't see him."

Chapter 19

Out of the corner of my eye, I watched the man crouch low to the ground and do his best duck-walk across the lawn. But his attempt to make himself invisible failed miserably, and I stifled a laugh and shook my head.

"Unbelievable," Josie whispered.

"Now?" I said.

"No, give him a few more seconds," she said.

Being downwind, we could easily hear the dogs' throaty growls, but the interloper continued his trek oblivious to their presence. When he was about twenty feet from the edge of the pool, Josie leaned forward in her chair.

"Okay, let's have some fun," she said, then called out. "Go get him, guys!"

All four house dogs hurled themselves off their lounge chairs and hit the ground running. The man spotted them and immediately turned tail and dashed for the gate. With one hand on his hat and the other on the camera hanging from his neck, he made a valiant effort to make it to safety. But it wasn't his night.

Chloe was the first to catch up to him, and she lowered her shoulder and hit the intruder low, just above his ankles. He stumbled, almost regained his balance, but eventually tumbled forward and fell face down on the lawn. Captain let loose with a final snarl then grabbed one of his ankles. The man kicked his leg frantically to get free, but the more he struggled, the tighter the Newfie's grip became.

"If you keep shaking your leg like that, he's going to assume you're a chew toy," Josie said as she approached.

"And that wouldn't be good," I said. "He goes through a couple a week."

"At least," Josie said, nodding as she continued to study the intruder sprawled out and surrounded by all four dogs.

"Get him off me," the man said, glaring up at us before falling silent when he spotted Al and Dente, two of the sweetest creatures on the planet, sitting on their haunches directly in front of him displaying impressive dental work while their guttural growls droned like background music in the breeze. "I thought Golden Retrievers were supposed to be gentle and loving."

"Oh, they are," Chef Claire said, reaching down to stroke their heads. "But they can be incredibly protective when they think their family is being threatened."

"I'm no threat."

"What are you doing here?" I said.

"I was just out for a walk and saw the lights were on. So, I thought I'd stop by and say hi."

"Anybody buying it?" Josie said, glancing around.

"Not for a second, dear," my mother said. "Hello, Geoffrey."

"Hi, Mrs. C.," the man said. "Nice night, huh?"

My mother pursed her lips then nodded to Josie.

"Captain," Josie said. "Squeeze."

"Ow," the man yelped when Captain applied more pressure to his ankle. "C'mon, Josie. Enough already. Get him off me."

"What are you doing here, Geoffrey?" my mother said. "As if I didn't already know."

"Okay, okay. You got me," he said. "Tell him to let go and I'll talk." Then he spotted the Premier standing behind my mother and gave him a small wave. "Hey, Gerald."

"Hello, Geoffrey," Gerald said, without emotion. "Looks like you've got yourself into a bit of a jam."

"Yeah, I forgot about the dogs," Geoffrey said.

"You've given me a great idea," Gerald said, laughing. "I think I'll bring these guys to my next press conference. That should keep the questions to a minimum."

"Your next press conference?" he said, frowning. "You mean the one where you'll be announcing your resignation?"

"Cheap shot," I snapped.

"Yeah," Josie said. "Totally uncalled for. Captain. Squeeze."

"Ow…ow. Geez, Josie. Knock it off. What the hell do you feed him?"

"Nosy reporters," Josie deadpanned.

"Well, get him off me. That frigging hurts."

"It's supposed to hurt," Josie said, then glanced at Gerald. "I think you're onto something with that press conference idea."

"Yes, I like it," Gerald said. "Okay, I think he's learned his lesson. Let him up."

"Yeah, it's time for a chat," Josie said, then reached down to stroke Captain's head. "Okay, Captain. Let go. C'mon, let him go. I know you'd like to chew that ankle for a while, but we need to have a word with him." She lowered her voice. "Let go. Now."

The Newfie grudgingly let go of the ankle then sat on his haunches without taking his eyes off the reporter. Geoffrey sat up, then used his hands to get to his feet. The dogs continued to surround him. They'd stopped growling but maintained intense stares as the reporter bent down to retrieve his hat and did his best to compose himself.

"Would you like a drink, Geoffrey?" my mother said.

"You read my mind, Mrs. C."

My mother began leading the way back to the table.

"Hold up a sec, Mom."

"What is it, darling?"

"Let me see that thing," I said, nodding at the impressive camera dangling from his neck.

"What do you want with my camera?" he said, frowning at me.

"Just let me see it. I've been thinking about getting one," I said, lying through my teeth.

He reluctantly handed it over and watched closely as I rolled it around in my hands.

“This is a telephoto lens, right?” I said.

“Maybe.”

Josie and I laughed. Then I began fiddling with the bottom of the camera.

“What are you doing?” Geoffrey said.

“Did you take any pictures before you came through the gate?” I said, studying his reaction. “I bet you could get pretty up close and personal with this lens.”

“Maybe a couple,” he said with a shrug.

“You should have quit while you were ahead,” Josie said. “Let me see that thing.”

I handed her the camera, and moments later, she had the back open. She reached inside and removed a small object I immediately recognized.

“Nice,” Josie said, examining the storage device. “How much memory does this thing have?”

“Sixty some gigs,” Geoffrey said.

“Are you good about backing up your work?” I said.

“Sure. Every night before I go to bed,” he said, then the penny dropped. “Why do you want to know?”

“We’d hate to ruin all your hard work, Geoffrey,” Josie said, then turned and fired the storage device into the deep end of the pool.

“Ah, Josie,” he said, scowling at her. “Those were exclusive photos.”

"Yes, I know," she said. "I guess you'll just have to use your memory. Okay, I'm ready for a cocktail. C'mon, Captain. Who's the good boy?" She reached down and gave him a solid thump on the side then raced the dog back to the table.

I handed Geoffrey his camera back and strolled off with Chloe bouncing at my feet.

"Nice tackle, Girl," I said, pausing briefly to bend down and stroke her head.

We all sat down, and Paulie grabbed a couple bottles of wine from the small fridge on the patio. He poured then sat down next to my mother and gently patted her thigh.

"And you were wondering what we were going to do all day," he said, laughing.

"Yes," my mother said, reaching for her wine. "It has been rather eventful, hasn't it?"

"How did you know I was here, Geoffrey?" Gerald said.

"I didn't," he said, then took a long swig of Pinot Grigio.

He glanced around at all four dogs. Al and Dente were sitting on either side of Chef Claire watching his every move. Captain was on his stomach, staring up at him as Josie continued to gently scratch his ears. Chloe had her front legs propped on my chair and was also keeping a close eye on our visitor. Queen, apparently unruffled by the interruption, was again stretched out on my mother's lap about to doze off.

"Do they really need to be here?" Geoffrey said, nodding at the dogs. "They make me nervous."

"Well, I hate to tell you, Geoffrey," Chef Claire said. "They're not going to go anywhere as long as you're here."

"Yeah," I said. "They can be pretty protective."

"Just don't make any sudden movements and you'll be fine," Josie deadpanned over the rim of her wine glass. "Isn't that right, Captain?"

The Newfie woofed once without taking his eyes off the reporter.

"How did you end up here?" my mother said, officially getting down to business.

"I took a shot," Geoffrey said with a shrug. "By the way, nice wild goose chase you led us on this afternoon. Well played."

"Thank you," my mother said, grinning at him. "When did you finally realize what was going on?"

"Right around the time you and the cops parked and entered the mall," Geoffrey said, rubbing his ankle. "I think he drew blood."

"Occupational hazard," Josie said, shrugging it off.

"I could sue you."

"Yeah, maybe," she said. "But would you do that before or after we had you arrested for breaking and entering?"

"What are you talking about? I merely walked through the gate."

"Really?" Josie said, glancing over at me. "My memory must be slipping."

"Mine too," I said. "The way I remember it is that we didn't even realize you were here until we saw you trying to pick the lock on the back door."

Geoffrey sat back and eventually nodded, conceding the point.

"Okay. Fair enough," he said, then held out his empty glass for Paulie to refill. He took a sip then continued. "After the mall, everyone headed off to camp out in front of Gerald's place."

"Are they still there?" Gerald said.

"I'd be surprised if they weren't," Geoffrey said. "I was there for about an hour, then I started thinking."

"Don't you hate when that happens?" I said.

"What?"

"Nothing. Continue."

"I decided you must be staying somewhere else," Geoffrey said. "And my first thought was you were probably staying with Mrs. C. You know, since you two are so tight, and you were at the police station all afternoon obviously waiting for Gerald to make bail." He paused to drink more wine. "And when I realized you weren't home, I took a shot and wandered down the beach. I guess I got lucky. Until I almost got eaten alive by that beast."

"You need to keep Gerald's whereabouts to yourself, Geoffrey," my mother said.

"What's in it for me?" the reporter said, then focused on the Premier. "I know you didn't kill that woman, Gerald. Somebody is trying to set you up for murder."

"Thank you. I appreciate that," Gerald said.

"But I've got a job to do. And this is the biggest story to hit the island in years."

"I'm very aware of both, Geoffrey," Gerald said, folding his arms across his chest as he studied the reporter. "What do you want?"

"I want exclusive rights to the story."

"We can't tell you the story yet. We're not even sure what the hell is going on."

"I can wait," Geoffrey said. "So, I'll keep my mouth shut about where you are, but I get sole, exclusive rights to the story when it finally shakes out."

"I can live with that," Gerald said.

"No," I said, shaking my head. "We need more."

"What?" the reporter said, staring at me. "Suzy, I don't work for a charitable organization. What else do you expect me to do?"

"Just play along, that's all," I said, rubbing my forehead. "We need you to participate in a little…targeted misdirection."

"You got any clue what she's talking about?" Gerald said to my mother.

"What do you think?" my mother said. "Okay, darling. What's on your mind?"

"You've got friends on the other side of the island, right?" I said to Gerald.

"I run the frigging government, Suzy. I've got friends everywhere."

"Yeah, I know," I said. "But who's your best buddy on the other side of the island?"

"Billy," Gerald said immediately. "Billy Unger."

"Do you trust him?"

"With my life," Gerald said.

"Okay, here's what we'll do," I said, leaning forward. "It's only a matter of time before more of Geoffrey's knucklehead colleagues wander down here."

"You want me to stay with Billy?"

"No, but we want everyone to think you're staying with him," I said, then sat back in my chair and addressed the table. "You need to call Billy and ask him to play along."

"That won't be a problem."

"Good. Geoffrey, tomorrow morning you're going to start spreading the rumor with other members of the press that you have it on good authority Gerald is staying with Billy at his place."

"Okay," Geoffrey said. "I suppose I can do that. As long as I get the exclusive."

"Yeah, you got it," Gerald said, then focused on me. "Is that all?"

"No, ask Billy to wander down his driveway and speak to the press for a few minutes after they show up. Have Billy grudgingly admit you're staying at his house, but you won't be available to take any questions, and he'd appreciate it if the press would respect Gerald's privacy...blah, blah, blah. You know the drill."

"Well done, darling," my mother said, beaming at me.

"Thanks, Mom."

"I like it," Gerald said. "And Billy's gonna love it. He hates the media. No offense, Geoffrey."

"I'm used to it," the reporter said. "Okay, I'm gonna get out of here. I have an early morning interview with the victim's parents."

"Really?" I said, perking up. "Where are you meeting them?"

Josie groaned softly when she heard my question.

"At Jimmy's office. They're finalizing the arrangements to fly Samantha's body back home."

"So, you've met them?" I said.

"Yeah, I managed to bump into them today," the reporter said.

"I bet," Josie said, shaking her head.

"Josie, it's what we do," Geoffrey said. "I'm not going to apologize for doing my job."

"Fair enough," Josie said, glancing across the table at me. "But let's remember they're in mourning. Try to be gentle with all your questions."

"I promise I'll be on my best behavior," Geoffrey said, getting to his feet.

"I wasn't talking to you."

Chapter 20

After a big breakfast, my mother and Paulie headed for the pool with Max, trailed closely by all four dogs. Josie and Chef Claire stretched out on lounge chairs to watch the always entertaining show while Gerald and I headed inside to wash the dishes. I studied him silently as I watched him wipe down one of the counters. Eventually, he caught my stare and leaned against the sink.

"What's on your mind, Suzy?"

"I'm just wondering how you're doing," I said, sitting down at the kitchen island.

"I'll be fine," he said with a shrug. "I've been in worse spots."

"I find that hard to believe."

"You worry too much," he said, waving me off.

"Okay. I'll let it go."

"Is it like this around here every morning?" he said, resuming his work.

"You mean, semi-organized chaos? Yeah, pretty much."

"It's nice. Not your typical family by any stretch of the imagination, but it works," he said. "And you guys seem to pull it off with no effort at all. It's a lot. Four dogs and a baby."

"Don't forget my mother," I deadpanned.

Gerald laughed and began loading the dishwasher.

"Shouldn't you be jogging?"

"I convinced Chef Claire we should take the day off," I said. "You know, given your situation."

"You used me as an excuse to get out of exercise?"

"Hey, you play the cards you're dealt, right?" I said, grinning at him.

His trademark booming laugh filled the kitchen.

"So, what's the plan for today?"

"Well, you're going to relax and stay out of sight. Josie and I are going to see if we can have a word with Samantha's parents before they leave the island. And hopefully, we'll be able to get some sort of idea about who is setting you up."

"By talking to her parents?" Gerald said.

"No, I doubt if they'll have much to offer," I said. "But maybe Jimmy or Detective Renfro have come up with something useful."

"Like what?"

"I don't have a clue, Gerald," I said, grabbing a sponge to wipe down the granite. "We need a bit of a breakthrough. Some piece of information. You know, like a missing piece of the puzzle to help make some sense of all this."

"It would be a whole lot easier if Little Billy were still alive," he said.

"Tell me about it," I said. "But he must have been working with someone down here. Probably whoever it was that took off with Quiver's dog. And I'm hoping whoever it is raises their ugly head at some point to tell you what they want."

"You mean, something like fifty million bucks?" Gerald said.

"Yeah, that would be a start," I said. "But even that wouldn't get you off the hook. You're directly tied to one murder with the possibility of a second charge heading your way. And when people start asking questions-"

"Which they already are," Gerald said.

"Yeah," I said, then began reciting from memory, working myself into a fever pitch in the process. "And if it comes to light you and Bentley had worked together to screw Slash Quivers, it's a short trip to follow that lead right to the hospital you built with the stolen fifty million. Combine that with the fact the old man's son was found dead on the beach, which we both know wasn't a suicide, *and* Samantha was found in the trunk of your car, *and* the police found the murder weapon at your house, *and* it's likely the murder weapon is going to match the one used to kill Bentley on his sailboat-"

"Suzy," Gerald said, interrupting again.

"What?"

"Do me a favor."

"Sure. What do you need?"

"Promise me you'll never become a motivational speaker. Or a prosecutor. Because I'm about to jump into the ocean wearing cement flippers," he said, exasperated. "Geez, enough already. I got it. I'm screwed."

"Not yet," I chirped, gently punching him on the shoulder. I glanced around the kitchen. "Okay, it looks great. We're done here." I headed out of the kitchen, then came to a stop in the doorway. "Did you call your buddy on the other side of the island?"

"I did," Gerald said, drying his hands. "He's in."

"Cool. Stay off the beach and out of sight today. Later."

My initial challenge of the day was to convince a stubborn Captain to get his butt into the backseat of Josie's jeep. Eventually, he complied with a throaty grumble and a couple of under his breath woofs at me.

"I told you he likes to ride shotgun," Josie said, backing out of the garage. "Top down, okay?"

"It's great," I said, enjoying the breeze as she headed for the main road. I glanced over my shoulder and spotted Captain staring back at me. He was sitting up and dominating the back seat. "It's nice back there, isn't it, Captain?"

The Newfie turned his head ninety degrees and looked out at the passing cars.

"He's ignoring me," I said, laughing. "The little bugger is actually pissed off at me."

"He'll get over it," Josie said, reaching back with one hand to rub his chest without taking her eyes off the road. "What's our first stop? The shelter or Jimmy's office?"

"Let's head to Jimmy's," I said. "I think he's meeting with Samantha's parents at the moment."

"Please, Suzy. I'm begging you. Be gentle with them."

"I'm not a total idiot," I said, then took a sip of coffee from my travel mug.

A few minutes later, Josie pulled into a parking spot directly in front of the building where Jimmy spent the majority of his workday. We climbed out and Captain led the way up the steps. Inside, we were greeted by a security guard who was a regular at the restaurant.

"Good morning, ladies," the guard said, coming out from behind his desk to welcome Captain. "Geez, Captain. You're getting so big. The last time I saw him, he was still growing."

"Hey, Bobby. It's okay to take him along, isn't it?" Josie said.

"Where you going?"

"Jimmy's office," she said.

"I can't imagine anybody in there is gonna complain," he said, scratching the Newfie's ears.

"Is that a dead person joke?" Josie said, frowning at him.

"It is," Bobby said, handing us a clipboard to sign in. "But apparently not a good one."

We headed down the hall with a wave and Captain hung close to Josie while continuing to ignore my presence.

"I can't believe his attitude," I said.

"You took his spot," Josie said, continuing her brisk pace.

"Yeah, and I also feed him, pet him, throw balls for him, give him baths, and dry him off when he gets out of the pool."

"I know. But you took his spot."

We came to a stop when we spotted a man and a woman exit Jimmy's office. The woman was sobbing and using a handful of tissues to stay on top of the tears streaming down her cheeks. The man gently held her elbow, but the look on his face sent chills up my spine. Bewildered anger was the closest description I could come up with, and his wild-eyed expression reminded me of a caged animal desperate for an escape route.

A wave of emotion surged through me, and I flashed back to the time when my husband, Max, had been killed on our honeymoon. And the memories of the event, and the subsequent months when I'd often wondered if the pain would ever subside produced a powerful wave of sympathy for the couple who had just lost their daughter. I couldn't even imagine how I'd react if anything tragic ever happened to my little girl. I took a step to one side to give them room to get by and merely nodded a greeting. I watched them head for the exit, and they soon disappeared from sight.

"You do know who that was, right?" Josie said, giving me a confused stare.

"I do," I said, blinking back tears. "They've got enough to worry about at the moment. The last thing they need is me asking them a bunch of questions."

Josie pulled me in for a long hug.

"I'm proud of you," she whispered.

"Okay," I said, exhaling loudly. "Let's go. We've got work to do."

I knocked softly and a voice invited us in. We entered the office and spotted Geoffrey sitting on a couch rubbing his temples. When he spotted Captain, he tucked his legs underneath him and kept a close eye on the Newfie who was already emitting a low, throaty growl.

"Keep that beast away from me."

"Relax, Geoffrey," Josie said. "He's a big baby."

"Tell that to my ankle," he said.

"Where's Jimmy?" I said.

"He's out back making sure everything is ready to go," Geoffrey said. "Samantha's parents are flying back with the body this afternoon."

"We saw them in the hall," I said.

"And?" he said, raising an eyebrow at me.

"And nothing," I said, shaking my head. "We didn't even try to talk with them."

"Probably a good call," he said. "That was the worst half-hour I've spent in a very long time."

"They're devastated," Josie said.

"Yeah, and I don't think Samantha's death is going to help the marriage," Geoffrey said, sliding his notebook into his shirt pocket.

"Why's that?" I said, leaning against the desk.

"It's pretty obvious they're on shaky ground," he said. "And they're dealing with her death very differently."

"He looked angry," I said.

"He's way past angry," the reporter said. "And his wrath is focused solely on his daughter."

"He's blaming her?" Josie said, surprised.

"Oh, yeah. He kept going on and on about her life choices. And every time her mom tried to redirect the conversation, he started yelling. Which made her cry even harder. Which I didn't think was possible." He shook his head. "I hate this part of the job."

"What did he say about her life choices?" I said, my interest piqued.

"He hated all of them," Geoffrey said. "Picked the wrong college, picked the wrong men. Passed up a chance to go to med school to become a medical officer. Something he considered to be a total waste of her talents. Samantha wouldn't settle down. She was much too impressionable. Wasted her time traveling when she should have been building a career and family. And her latest choice, one that sent her old man off the deep end, was her decision to come down here and then sail off into the sunset to Cuba with a complete stranger."

"Cuba?" I said.

"That's what her old man said," Geoffrey said.

"Did they talk about this mysterious stranger?" I said.

"Not a lot. It sounded like it was her new boyfriend."

"He lived down here?"

"That would be my guess," he said with a shrug. "I don't think Samantha had worked up the courage to introduce him to her parents. It was pretty clear they didn't approve."

"Her boyfriend had to be Quiver's partner," I said, scratching the back of my head. "You know, the guy he was working with down here trying to..."

"Trying to do what?" the reporter said, immediately on point.

"Uh, trying to set Gerald up. What else?" I said, silently cursing myself for almost divulging the missing fifty million to a reporter.

"Well, I guess we'll never know, huh?" Geoffrey said, getting off the couch while keeping a close eye on Captain. "I wish it was five o'clock."

"Why's that?" Josie said.

"Because I'd be able to have a stiff drink and try to forget about this morning," he said, heading for the door.

"Are you going to get the rumor about Gerald started?" I said.

"Just as soon as I can get out of here. Did Gerald call his buddy?"

"He did. They're all set."

"Okay," he said, departing with a wave and a final glance at the Newfie who continued to watch him closely. "Let the games begin."

"You ready to head to the shelter?" Josie said.

"Let's hang here for a few minutes," I said, sitting down on the couch. "I'd like to have a quick word with Jimmy."

"Sure," she said, sitting down next to me and making room for Captain who hopped up on the couch and plopped his head in her lap. "Cuba. Why Cuba?"

"It's close," I said with a shrug. "And it's probably not a bad place to go if you don't want to be found."

"But what would Quiver's partner need to hide from? It's obvious they've got Gerald in a box. And Samantha's out of the way."

"I have no idea," I said, then we both looked up when the door on the other side of the office opened and Jimmy entered. He flinched when he spotted us. "Geez, I leave a reporter and grieving parents in my office, and when I come back, I find you two. It's definitely an upgrade."

"How you doing, Jimmy?" I said.

"Actually, a little mediocre today," he said. "I hate those conversations. There is absolutely nothing you can do or say that's going to help them heal."

"Yeah," I whispered.

"Hey, Captain," Jimmy said, kneeling down. "How's the big guy doing?"

Captain hopped off the couch and was soon on his back reveling in the vigorous tummy rub Jimmy was giving him.

"Is there something you guys need or did you just stop by to enjoy my magnetic personality?"

"Magnetic?" Josie said. "We must have a different definition."

"Ouch," he said, with a laugh then gave Captain a final scratch before hopping up and sitting on his desk. "What do you need?"

"Nothing, really," I said. "I was just wondering if you've found anything else out."

"As in, anything that might help Gerald duck a murder charge?"

"Yeah."

"Nah, I got nothing," he said. "Cause of death is confirmed. No other mitigating factors. I'm afraid I can't help you there."

"That's what I figured," I said.

"But there is something you can do for me," he said, hopping off the desk. "You guys mind giving me a hand with those boxes? Samantha was a nice woman, but she was lousy about keeping the place tidy. I need to take them out to storage."

"Sure," Josie said.

We followed him to the other side of the office. Jimmy pointed at a small box on the floor.

"Grab that one, Josie," he said. "It's not heavy. It's the last of Samantha's personal effects she had here. I'm putting it on the flight with her today."

"No problem," Josie said, bending down to pick it up.

"Those others look heavy," I said, staring down at the floor.

"They are," he said. "Don't worry, I'll get those."

"Then what can I do?" I said.

"Grab that urn from the shelf," Jimmy said, pointing before bending down to lift one of the boxes.

"Is that Quiver?" I said, frowning at him.

"It is," he said, adjusting the box in his arms. "But don't worry, he won't bite."

"Funny," I said, reaching on my tiptoes for the urn.

I grabbed it, settled back on my feet then did a half-turn. I took one step then fell forward stumbling when the tip of my shoe hit Captain's side who was stretched out on the floor directly behind me. I lifted my other foot to avoid stepping on him and completely lost my balance in the process. Three awkward steps later, I fell facedown on the floor, dropping the urn in the process. The lid popped off and moments later the office was filled with ash that swirled then slowly drifted down onto the tile floor.

"Uh, oh," I said, staring around at the mess. "Sorry about that, Little Billy."

"Smooth," Josie said, shaking her head at me.

"Shut it. I didn't see him there."

"Sure, that's completely understandable," she deadpanned. "He only weighs a hundred and fifty pounds."

"Geez, Suzy," Jimmy said, glaring at me. "Even the dead can't get any peace and quiet when you're around."

"I'm so sorry, Jimmy," I said, glancing around for something to use to clean the tile floor. "You got a vacuum cleaner? Maybe a Dustbuster?

"How about a broom and dustpan?" he said.

"Sure," I said with a shrug. "A little low-tech, but that'll work." Then I glanced down at something hanging out of Captain's mouth. "Hey, Jimmy?"

"Yeah?"

"Are there supposed to be bones in these ashes?" I said.

"Bones? Not unless somebody botched the cremation."

"How do you botch a cremation?" Josie said.

"Basically, by not running the furnace long enough," Jimmy said, then focused on me. "Why do you ask?"

I nodded at Captain and did my best not to laugh at the piece of protruding bone and nonchalant expression on his face that seemed to be saying, 'there's nothing to see here.'

"Oh, Captain," Josie said, kneeling in front of the dog. "Drop that. I said, drop it."

The Newfie slowly lowered his head and placed the bone on the floor. Then he woofed once, obviously annoyed at her for taking away his snack. Jimmy grabbed a tissue then slipped the bone into an evidence bag.

"Yuk," he said with a frown. "He's a bit of a slobberer, isn't he?"

"Hey," Josie said, scowling at him. "That's my dog you're talking about."

"Why on earth would there still be bones?" I said, grabbing the broom he handed me.

"Like I said," Jimmy said. "Somebody neglected to run the process to completion."

"Who handles it?" I said.

"George Sanders."

"He runs the funeral home next door, right?" I said.

"Yeah, and he has a crematorium we use when we need it," Jimmy said. "But he always does a great job. Let me give him a call. Hopefully, he's in the office and not out playing golf."

I continued to sweep and ignore the dirty look Josie was giving me. When I had the ashes in a pile, Josie knelt down holding the dustpan. Then she carefully poured and tapped them back into the urn.

"Unbelievable," she said under her breath.

"Hey, it could have happened to anybody."

"I seriously doubt that."

"Stuff a sock in it," I said, then knelt down next to Captain and gently rubbed his side. "Are you okay? I'm sorry I tripped over you, Captain."

The Newfie got up and draped his front paws on my shoulders then licked the side of my face. I gave him a long hug.

"I told you he'd forgive you," Josie said, laughing.

Jimmy ended his call with a deep frown etched on his face.

"That was weird," he said.

"What's the matter?" I said, continuing to hug and pet Captain.

"George didn't do the cremation."

"Who did?" I said.

"Samantha."

"Huh? Was she qualified to do that?"

"How hard can it be?" Josie said. "Flip the switch and wait until it's done, right?"

"I'm pretty sure there's a bit more to it," Jimmy said.

"Why didn't George handle it?" I said.

"Because Samantha came to his office and told him she had a tee time at the North Sound Club she couldn't use," Jimmy said, still frowning.

"But it was getting close to tee time, and if George wanted to make it, he needed to leave right away," I said.

"Yeah. Son of a gun."

"She told him she would handle the cremation for him," I said.

"She did," Jimmy said. "She told George she'd done it before. So, he quickly walked her through the process, then headed for the course."

"Could George get in any trouble for doing that?" Josie said.

"Well, it's probably not the smartest business decision he could have made, but I doubt if anybody would lose any sleep over it. It really couldn't hurt anything. The guy was already dead, right?"

"Yeah," I said, my mind racing. Then I flinched and shook my head to clear the cobwebs.

"Uh-oh," Josie said.

"What's the matter?" Jimmy said.

"She's got the look," Josie said. "Where on earth are you going?"

"I need to make a phone call," I said. "You go on ahead to the shelter. I'll catch a cab back to the house."

"You mind explaining yourself before you leave?" Josie said.

"Later," I said. "I've got some stuff to sort out first." Then I glanced at Jimmy and nodded at the evidence bag on his desk. "Don't let that bone out of your sight."

Chapter 21

I walked outside into bright sunlight and slipped my sunglasses on before I did my best lumber out of the parking lot and down the street to a nearby coffee shop. I found a quiet spot in the back, ordered a cappuccino and a muffin then made the call.

"Hello, Suzy."

"How did you know it was me?" I said, surprised.

"Because I'm a master of my craft. A technician of the highest order who constantly stays on top of the latest and greatest advancements in technology. And someone who others believe is somehow in touch with the enormous universe we dwell within," Agent Tompkins said.

"Funny."

"And your number shows up on my screen when you call."

"Oh, that's right. Duh," I said. "How are you doing?"

"I'm busy. What do you want?"

"I need a favor," I said. "Actually, now that I think about it, we might be doing each other a favor."

"I'm not falling for that again."

"Where's the trust, Agent Tompkins?" I said, laughing. "C'mon, it'll be fun. You're gonna like this one."

"Suzy, I'm swamped. I'm sorry, but I couldn't possibly take care of whatever you need for at least a week."

"A week? Geez, Agent Tompkins, people down here already calling for Gerald's resignation."

"A murder charge will do that to a politician," he said.

"Maybe two."

Agent Tompkins fell silent for several moments before continuing.

"You confirmed Gerald was in Barbados when Bentley got shot?"

"Yeah, he was giving a speech at some conference. But Gerald said he never left the hotel."

"What did you expect him to say?" Agent Tompkins said. "That's not good news."

"When are the ballistics coming back on that one?" I said, preparing myself for the worst.

"Actually, I haven't gotten around to asking for the bullet yet," he said softly.

"What? Why not?"

"Like I said, I've been busy."

"Horse pucky," I said, then the penny dropped. "Holy crap. You're slow-walking this one. Aren't you?"

"Maybe."

"Son of a gun," I said. "I gotta ask."

"I'd be shocked if you didn't. I've been doing a little research on Gerald. And he just doesn't fit the pattern. I don't think the guy is capable of hurting a squirrel, much less kill two people. And as much as it sometimes pains me to say it, I trust your instincts."

"Thank you, Agent Tompkins. I appreciate that. Whoever said the FBI doesn't have a heart?"

"Don't spread it around, okay?"

"No, I'm serious. Thank you."

"You're welcome. But that doesn't change the fact I'm incredibly busy, Suzy."

"I see one of Chef Claire's cakes in your future," I said in a singsong voice.

"You really think you can bribe an FBI agent with a cake?"

I stayed quiet and waited it out.

"German chocolate?" he said eventually.

"That's the one."

"I do love that cake."

"I know you do," I said, slowly reeling him in. "What do you say?"

"I'll do it for two," Agent Tompkins said.

"You greedy little bugger. You want two cakes?"

"I do. One for me to eat at my house. And another to bring into the office. And I want them sent FedEx. No seven-day ground delivery where they'll get stale."

"Should I send a carton of milk along?" I said, shaking my head.

"No, I can handle that part," he said. "We got a deal?"

"We do," I said.

"Okay. What do you need?"

"I need a DNA analysis run as fast as you can make it happen," I said, then got ready for the questions.

"DNA analysis? What the hell are you up to down there, Suzy?"

"I think we had a breakthrough today," I said, then proceeded to tell him the highlights of my visit to Jimmy's office. I had to pause a couple of times to wait out his laughter. When I finished, I rubbed my forehead, doing everything I could to shake off the headache that was emerging.

"I can't believe you tripped over Josie's Newfie. I would have loved to have seen that."

"Are you done?" I said, doing my best to stay patient until another round of laughter subsided.

"Yeah, I'm done. So, you want a DNA test run on one of Quiver's bones?"

"I do. I think it's part of his foot," I said. "Does that matter?"

"Only to Quiver."

"Funny. Can you do it?"

"Sure, we do them all the time," he said. "But I do have to ask you a simple question. Why on earth do you want to run a DNA test on a dead guy?"

I took a few deep breaths to prepare myself for the words about to come out of my mouth.

"Because I don't think those are Quiver's ashes."

"Okay," Agent Tompkins said with a chuckle. "You got me again. I did not see that one coming. And whose ashes do you think they might be?"

"I have no idea," I said. "But that's not the point. What matters is I think Little Billy Quiver is alive and well."

"He faked his own death?" Agent Tompkins said. "C'mon, Suzy. Do you have any idea how hard that is to do?"

"I could probably ballpark it," I said, squinting as my headache worsened. "But if you were working in concert with a local medical officer, you could probably figure out a way to make it happen, right?"

He fell silent, and I popped a small handful of aspirin and washed them down with a sip of cappuccino while I waited.

"Well, since we're talking about the islands and the way they're sometimes a little loose with standard procedures…and if there weren't too many prying eyes around at the time, I suppose it's possible."

"Samantha was the one who confirmed Little Billy was dead after we found him on the beach. And she had the paramedics take him straight to the morgue."

"Okay, the plot thickens," he said. "Anything else?"

"Aren't their drugs you can take to slow your heart rate down? You know, to make your pulse weak."

"There are," he said. "And they've been used before in cases like this."

"And when Samantha got the body back to the morgue, she would have used another drug to counteract the one Quiver game himself on the beach," I said.

"That's the way it's supposed to work," Agent Tompkins said. "But it's a dangerous game to play with your body."

"Desperate times call for desperate measures. Do you guys have Quiver's DNA on file?" I said, dreading the answer.

"Are you kidding?" Agent Tompkins said, laughing. "We've probably got a whole wing devoted to the Quiver family. I'm sure we've got it."

"That's great," I said. "Tomorrow?"

"Tomorrow? That's asking a lot, Suzy."

"The day after tomorrow?"

"I'll see what I can do," he said. "So, you think Quiver is the one who killed the medical officer?"

"I am," I said. "You want to hear my theory on that one?"

"Do I have a choice?"

"Did you take a funny pill today, Agent Tompkins? I think when Quiver finally found out about the fifty million his old man had stashed away down here, he came looking for it. And he somehow put it together it was Gerald and Bentley who were responsible for taking it. So, after Quiver got rid of Bentley in Barbados, he decided to set Gerald up. And after he faked his death, and Samantha had finished her part of the plan, he shot her and pinned it on Gerald."

"And how did Quiver actually find this Samantha?" Agent Tompkins said.

"I think he went looking for an impressionable young woman who had the appropriate background. Then he orchestrated her making friends with Jimmy. She offered to cover for him whenever he went on vacation, and Quiver was just sitting back, biding his time."

"Do you have any concept about the degree of premeditation and patience a plan like that would require?"

"Well, he did spend twenty years trying to find the money," I said. "That's a lot of time to come up with something clever."

"Clever? I think the word you're looking for is diabolical. Not to mention, despicable."

"Look, I know it sounds weird, Agent Tompkins. But we're talking about fifty million bucks."

"Yeah, I get it. And that's a boatload of money. But it still sounds like a major stretch, Suzy. You're making a whole lot of assumptions."

"I know," I said. "But I think I'm onto something."

"Where did this all come from?" Agent Tompkins said.

"It was something her father said to a local reporter during an interview today," I said. "Samantha's dad is obviously devastated by her death, but he's also very angry. At one point, he told the reporter he couldn't believe his daughter was crazy enough to sail off into the sunset to Cuba with a complete stranger."

"Cuba? Now, that's interesting," he said.

"Does the U.S. have an extradition treaty with Cuba?"

"Technically, yes. But we know a lot of cases where some of the folks we're looking for have been able to grease the right palms. For the right amount of money, I'm sure it's possible to find sanctuary down there."

"Do you know how far it is from Grand Cayman to Cuba?"

"Do I look like a travel agent? Geez, Suzy, you're the one who lives down there."

"Just Google it."

"Huh? How about that?"

"What is it?"

"I must have missed the memo."

"The memo?" I said, frowning.

"Yeah, the memo announcing the fact I was now working for you," he snapped.

"I'm sorry, Agent Tompkins. My brain's on fire at the moment."

"Thanks for the warning," he said above the sound of his keyboard clacking. "Okay, here we go. Well, if he were to land on the west end of Cuba, it's around two hundred and fifty miles. Give or take."

"What would that be from a sailing perspective? Three days, maybe two with the right wind?"

"And perfect weather and calm water," he said. "I'd say three at a minimum to be safe."

"That means he'll be landing soon," I said. "Probably sometime tomorrow."

"If your wild guess turns out to be right, that sounds close."

"The Bureau has people down there, right?"

For some reason, he found the question funny, and he laughed long and hard.

"People assigned to Cuba? Yeah, we might have a couple down there."

"Okay, well played. I deserved that one."

"I just had another thought," he said. "If the guy couldn't get his hands on the old man's money, what's he doing for cash?"

"Well, you said yourself he's been a criminal forever."

"Yeah, he must have some money stashed somewhere," Agent Tompkins said. "Still, it would be risky to use banks or credit cards."

I gave it some thought, then an idea bubbled to the surface.

"The foundation. The guy had some sort of foundation."

"This foundation have a name?"

I searched my memory bank, and my earlier conversation with Detective Renfro came back in bits and pieces.

"The Quiver Society," I said.

"Catchy name. Okay, I'll check it out," he said.

"So, you're starting to believe I'm onto something?"

"No," he said with a chuckle. "I just want to cover all my bases. I have a feeling I'm going to be retelling this story for years, and I want to make sure I've got all the details straight."

"Okay, have your fun. But when it turns out I'm right, you're gonna owe me dinner."

"Suzy, if you're right about this, I promise I'll make it my personal mission to hunt this guy down. You're going to send me that bone today?"

"I am. It'll be coming FedEx."

"Perfect," he said, then paused before continuing. "Just not with the cakes, right?"

Chapter 22

Given the fact I needed some peace and quiet to sort out the collection of jumbled thoughts rolling around my head, I climbed into the back seat of a taxi and did my best to appear preoccupied. It wasn't much of a challenge. Mercifully, the driver wasn't in a chatty mood, and we rode in silence all the way back to the house. Grateful for his ability to keep quiet, I overtipped him then headed inside where I found everyone sprawled around the living room killing a few hours until it was time to start making dinner plans.

I shivered then grabbed my sweatshirt off the back of a chair and pulled it on. I looked at my mother sitting on the floor with Max between her legs playing with Chloe, who kept nudging a tennis ball toward the baby. Max giggled with delight as she did her best to roll the ball back. My mother noticed my stare and frowned up at me.

"Is there a problem, darling?"

"If you miss the cold that much, Mom, why don't you just head back to Clay Bay and catch the last of the winter?"

"Perish the thought," she said.

"It's freezing in here. What on earth do you have the AC set on?"

"I was worried Max might have gotten overheated while she was outside earlier," my mother said.

"So, you thought frostbite was a better option?" I said, getting up to adjust the thermostat.

"Your mother thinks she's so funny, doesn't she?' my mother cooed to Max as she nuzzled her neck.

I sat back down, then the one thing I'd forgotten to do came back to me.

"Oh, crap. I forgot to call the Inn today."

"I called a couple of hours ago," Josie said, glancing up from the book she was reading.

"Is everything okay?"

"Cold, but good," she said. "Fifteen below and dropping."

"Yuk," I said. "Did you talk to Lacie?"

"No, she took the afternoon off to go snowmobiling with Rooster," Josie said. "I talked to Jill. Everything's fine."

"Snowmobiling in fifteen below," I said, shaking my head. "Unbelievable."

"You used to do it all the time, darling."

"Yeah, but that was back in the day before I knew any better."

Captain finished the loud drink he'd been having in the kitchen then padded back into the living room and stretched out at Paulie's feet.

"Did you hear that?" Josie said.

"I didn't hear anything," I said.

"Exactly. No clickety-clack of his nails on the tile," Josie said, nodding at the Newfie.

"Did he behave while you were cutting them?" I said.

"We had our moments," Josie said. "He's still not talking to me. Are you, Captain?"

The Newfie ignored her and draped his head over one of Paulie's feet.

"Don't forget who feeds you," Josie said in mock anger.

"Okay, darling," my mother said. "You said you had something to tell us. Why don't you get started?"

I draped a leg over my knee to scratch a mosquito bite on my foot then looked at Gerald who was sitting next to Chef Claire on the couch across from Josie.

"I think we might have had a breakthrough today," I said.

"Really?" Gerald said, leaning forward with an expectant look.

"But I need you to wait until I finish before you start jumping in," I said, raising a finger. "As soon as I start talking, you're probably going to think I need a nice, long vacation in a padded room."

"Oh, we're way past that," Josie deadpanned.

I waited out the laughter then nodded.

"Okay, I asked for that one," I said. "But I'm serious. It's gonna sound weird."

I launched into my story about our trip to Jimmy's office that morning, paused to wait out the laughter when I got to the part about how I'd managed to trip over Captain and spill what was left of Little Billy Quiver all over the office. I finished up with a summary of my conversation with Agent Tompkins and my theories as they stood at the moment.

As I told the story, everyone's expressions morphed from mild interest to anticipation to bewilderment. I knelt down and lifted Max into my arms, and she played with my nose while I waited for questions.

"Maybe we could put the padding in her bedroom," Chef Claire said. "You know, so she wouldn't have to travel."

"That works," Josie said, playing along before focusing on me. "All that happened after you left Jimmy's office?"

"Yeah," I whispered, gently jiggling Max in my arms.

"Okay, who wants first crack?" my mother said, glancing around.

"You go right ahead," Paulie said. "I'm still trying to get past the part where Captain tried to eat the evidence."

Gerald sat back and rested his chin on his hands.

"If you're right, and if you are, I'm personally going to nominate you for sainthood, how on earth could Quiver possibly believe anybody would piece all this together?"

"He doesn't need anybody to piece it all together," I said, jiggling Max more vigorously as another wave of thoughts collided.

"Suzy, if you keep bouncing Max like that, she's gonna lose her lunch," Josie said softly. "Sit down and try to relax."

"What do you mean?" Gerald said, totally focused on me.

"He only needs one murder to make this work," I said, heeding Josie's advice and sitting down next to her. I set Max on my knee, and she gurgled contentedly as she surveyed the scene. "If the cops had charged you with his supposed murder, all the better. But I think him staging his death was just a way to keep himself off the radar. His big play was Samantha. And if a link between you and Bentley were ever made, that would just be the icing on the cake." The cake reference jogged my memory, and I looked at Chef Claire. "Oh, before I forget, you need to make Agent Tompkins two of your German chocolate cakes."

"I do?" Chef Claire said with a frown. "Since when?"

"Since this afternoon. I cut a deal with him to expedite the DNA analysis."

Chef Claire shook her head and looked at Josie who shrugged back.

"It could have been worse," Josie said. "She could have negotiated away your feminine virtue."

"Oh," I said. "They need to be shipped FedEx. Apparently, he's got a thing about freshness."

"Amateur," Josie said.

"Yeah."

"I'll get right on it," Chef Claire deadpanned.

"Sorry," I said. "But I was in a jam. I'll pay you back."

"You can count on it," Chef Claire said, then laughed and shook her head again.

"How long is it going to take to get the DNA results back?" Gerald said.

"Well, he'll get the bone tomorrow. Maybe the next day or the day after. It probably depends on how much I bug him."

"Leave the man alone, darling. He's already going the extra mile."

"An extra mile?" Chef Claire said. "What a great idea, Mrs. C."

"Crap," I grunted under my breath.

"But even if we find out Quiver is alive and well, how is that, by itself, going to prove my innocence?" Gerald said.

"It's not," I said.

"There's always a catch," Josie said, gently lifting Max off my knee and holding her up in the air. "Isn't there, Max?"

"Do you have any suggestions about how I might clear my name?" Gerald said.

"I do," I said. "We're gonna need his confession. Preferably on tape."

"Sure," Gerald said, staring at me in disbelief. "And all I need to break seventy is an extra sixty yards off the tee and a magic putter."

"It won't be that hard, Gerald," I said.

"You want me to go to Cuba and beat a confession out of him?"

"No, I want you to coax a confession out of him," I said.

"In Cuba?"

"No, silly. Here."

"He's coming back to Grand Cayman?" Gerald said, thoroughly confused.

"Of course, he is."

"Why would he do that?" the Premier said.

"To get his money."

"But I don't have his money, Suzy."

"I know that, Gerald," I said, my voice rising. "But he doesn't. C'mon, work with me here."

Gerald focused his stare on my mother.

"What did you feed her when she was a kid?"

"I'm afraid her issues transcend diet, Gerald," my mother said. "Okay, darling. I'll play. How on earth do you plan on enticing Little Billy Quiver back to Grand Cayman?"

"With this," I said, removing a slip of paper from my shorts. "I jotted it down on the taxi ride home." I glanced at Gerald as I handed him the note. "I think it's pretty good, but feel free to make any changes you see fit."

"Okay, Little Billy, you win. It's time to call off the dogs. I have your money," Gerald said, reading the note aloud.

"Nice," Josie said, nodding her approval.

"Yes," Chef Claire said. "And remarkably concise."

"Aren't you sweet," I said, beaming back and forth at them. "But don't think for a second I missed the condescending tone." I focused on Gerald. "All we need to do is wait for Agent

Tompkins to confirm he's alive and landed in Cuba. Then come up with a way to get the note delivered."

"Just like that?" Gerald said.

"Pretty much," I said with a shrug. "We just need to find somebody willing to deliver it."

"I can handle that," Gerald said. "Not that I think it's going to be necessary."

"You think I'm way off base, don't you?"

"Actually, I was thinking more about left field. But yeah, let's say I have my doubts."

"That's okay," I said, grinning at him. "You'll see. You'll all see."

"Okay, enough of that," Josie said. "We'll stick a pin in this one until we hear back from Agent Tompkins."

"Fair enough," I said.

"So, moving on to more pressing issues," Josie said. "Are we going to cook tonight or should we just head to the restaurant?"

"Restaurant," everyone said unison.

"No," I said, remembering as I shook my head. "We can't do that."

"We can do anything we want," Josie said. "We own the place, remember?"

"Yes, but we're also hiding Gerald from prying eyes," I said. "We can't leave him here by himself."

“You’re right,” Josie said, hopping off the couch and heading to the kitchen.

“Where on earth is she going?” my mother said.

“To get the take out menu,” Chef Claire said.

Chapter 23

I headed back outside and sat down at the table where everyone had finished their dinners and were on break before dessert.

"She's out like a light," I said, reaching for my wine glass.

"She's about ready to take her first steps, darling."

"I think you're right, Mom. It's a bit early, but she's very close."

"Lucky you're on a fitness program," Chef Claire said.

"Don't remind me," I said. "Extra mile, huh?"

"Oh, you can count on it," she said with an evil grin.

The front gate swung open and Detective Renfro came into view. The dogs spotted him, made a mad dash across the lawn, then began wagging their tails vigorously as soon as they recognized him. He spent a few minutes saying hello, then approached the table.

"I got your text and thought I'd stop by on my way home," he said, sliding into the chair next to me. "Good evening, all."

"How are you, Detective?" Gerald said.

"I'm good. How are you holding up, sir?"

"I guess we'll find out soon," he said.

"I'm sorry," Detective Renfro said, confused by the comment. Then he spotted the three untouched entrees still in their takeout boxes sitting amid our empty plates. "You let Josie order, didn't you?"

"Yeah," I said to Chef Claire. "We really need to stop doing that."

"Help yourself, Detective Renfro," Chef Claire said. "I think there's a couple of steaks left. And an order of that fish curry you like."

"Well, I'd hate to see it go to waste," he said, looking through the selection.

"Not a chance," Josie said as she poured wine for the detective and topped off everyone's glass.

"Have you spoken with your attorney today?" Detective Renfro said.

"No, I've had my phone off all day," Gerald said. "Why?"

"The judge set your preliminary hearing for Friday," Detective Renfro said.

"Oh, great," Gerald said, grabbing his phone and turning it on. He waited for it to boot up then shook his head. "A dozen missed messages. I better give him a call." He got up from the table and headed inside.

Detective Renfro selected the fish curry and began eating. He took a couple of big bites, then swallowed and nodded.

"Fantastic. I'm starving. Haven't eaten all day," he said, then wiped his mouth. "What did you need to see me about?"

"This is gonna take some time. So, you keep eating while I talk."

"You don't have to ask twice," he said, picking up his utensils. "It's incredible."

I began telling him the story and went into considerable detail. In a couple of places, it sounded strange, even to me, but I pushed forward. At one point, Josie and Chef Claire, sitting nearby, both started laughing.

"The Captain part gets funnier every time she tells it," Chef Claire said.

"Yeah, I wish I'd had my camera with me," Josie said.

I glared at them briefly but continued to tell my story. I finished with a flourish and sat back in my chair with a proud grin fixed in place. Detective Renfro finished eating at the same time I stopped talking, and he took a sip of water and wiped his mouth.

"Interesting. One question," he said.

"Sure. Go right ahead," I said.

"If I say I believe you, do I get a cake, too?"

Josie and Chef Claire both cackled loudly, and I muttered a string of expletives under my breath then looked out over the pool.

"Sorry, I couldn't resist," Detective Renfro said. "Suzy, it's a fascinating theory."

"Do you buy it?" I said, staring at him.

"It's a lot to buy, Suzy," he said, shaking his head. "I saw the guy on the beach, remember?"

"I do. But you said yourself you were getting a pulse."

"A very weak and irregular one," he said.

"But after Samantha told us he was gone, we never checked him again," I said.

"Why would we?" he said, shrugging. "She was a medical officer."

"Exactly," I said, snapping my fingers. "And that was a brilliant part of their plan."

"I don't know," he said, scowling. "But it doesn't matter what I think right now, does it? We'll know soon enough." He turned to Chef Claire. "Now, about that cake."

"What about it?" she said.

"Do I get one?"

"Why on earth would you get a cake?" Chef Claire said.

"Well, let's call it hardship pay," he said, nodding in my direction.

"Funny," I grunted.

"Sure, I get that," Chef Claire said, shrugging. "Why not? It's just as easy to make three as it is two. I'll make you a cake, Detective Renfro."

"Thank you, Chef Claire." He grinned at me. "As long as you have that cake up your sleeve as a negotiating tactic, I'll be happy to listen to all the hairbrained theories you can come up with."

"Yeah, thanks. I'll keep that in mind."

My mother arrived with a tray of desserts and set it on the table in front of us.

"Did you check on Max while you were inside?" I said.

"She's sound asleep," my mother said, sitting down next to the detective. "Did she tell you her story?"

"She did," Detective Renfro said, eyeing the dessert selection.

"And?"

"It's a lot to digest," he said.

"Watch and learn, Detective," Josie said, reaching for a slice of lemon cake.

"I was referring to Suzy's theory," he said.

"Oh, never mind," she said, then got to work on her dessert.

"What do you think, Mrs. C.?" Detective Renfro said.

"I think she's right," my mother said.

"Thanks, Mom."

"And she better be right," my mother said, digging into her cake. "There's a lot riding on it."

"Don't worry, Mom. Gerald's not going to prison."

"Oh, I'm very aware of that, darling," she said, slowly chewing. "Perhaps a location without extradition, but certainly not prison."

"I'm going to pretend I didn't hear that," Detective Renfro said.

"Hear what?" my mother said, raising an eyebrow.

"Exactly," Detective Renfro said. "This lemon cake is excellent."

Chapter 24

The next two days crawled forward like a snail on sedatives. Determined to stay busy and keep my mind off the issue that remained top of mind, I'd made the decision to fill each day with mundane activities until I heard back from Agent Tompkins. The first day, I sailed to success with my goal of managing to stay busy. Concerning the other objective of keeping my mind off Gerald's situation, I failed miserably. And halfway through our morning run on day two, I gave up all hope and untethered my neurons and let them run wild.

Ten minutes later, I added headache to the list of exercise-induced maladies I was dealing with.

Proving to be a woman of her word, Chef Claire did add a mile to our daily routine. An extra mile doesn't sound like much if the majority of your experience with distance comes from driving. But sitting in a car watching the mile markers come and go is a lot different from plodding over soft sand that fills your running shoes and threatens to rip your calves off. By the time we finally reached the path that led up to the house, late morning of the second day, I was aching and exhausted. And given my loud tirade during the final quarter-mile, out of fresh expletives.

"The mouth on you," Chef Claire said, coming to a stop, barely out of breath. "And stop checking your phone."

"He should have called by now," I said, sliding my phone back into my running shorts.

"He's probably dealing with a coup or some sort of uprising," she said, sliding into a split and stretching. Then she stuck her hands in the sand, pushed herself into the air, and extended her legs in front of her at a ninety-degree angle. She maintained that position as she twisted her torso back and forth until I heard a soft pop when a vertebrae slid back in place. "Ah, that's better. I needed that." Then she caught the bewildered stare I was giving her. "What's the matter?"

"Does your species have a name? Where do you come from? A planet of alien gymnasts?"

"You should give it a try," she said, stretching out in the sand and propping herself up on her elbows.

"Now that's funny," I said. "I'd rather bungee jump naked into crocodile-infested waters."

"Whatever floats your boat, Suzy."

"What's gonna float my boat is a shower and then some pool-time with Max."

"Works for me," she said, climbing to her feet.

"You working tonight?" I said.

"No, they seem to be handling things great on their own."

"It's about time," I said. "This is supposed to be your quiet time of year. You're still working too hard."

"It's what I do," she said with a shrug. "But today is for relaxing. Maybe an afternoon matinee."

I followed her up the path fighting the onset of a leg cramp the entire way. We spotted Max sitting on the top step of the pool between my mother and Gerald. The dogs were in the deep end trying to cope with the onslaught of tennis balls Josie kept tossing into the water.

"Geez, Al. Captain. What the hell?" Josie called out. "There are a dozen balls in there. Why on earth do you have to fight over the same one?"

Captain reached out a massive paw and dunked the Golden and held him down until he managed to get loose. Al surfaced and retaliated by grabbing and tugging one of Captain's ears. Josie held up both hands in mock surrender and headed in our direction.

"Good job," I said. "Tire them out early."

"Yeah," Josie said. "I thought I'd try the same strategy Chef Claire has been using with you."

I waited out the laughter then sat down on the top step and lifted Max into my arms. I gently poked her arm to test for coloration.

"We should get her out of the sun," I said. "She's getting a little red."

"We were just heading in," my mother said. "We thought we'd spend the day binging something on TV."

"Yeah," Gerald said. "I'm feeling lazy. And I could use something to take my mind off things. Any word yet?"

"Nope," I said, again checking my phone for messages.

"Relax, darling. He'll call as soon as he has something. And we still have a few days before the arraignment."

"Is the press still camped out at your buddy's place?" I said.

"Oh, yeah. Apparently, they're working in shifts," Gerald said with a booming laugh.

"Geez," I said, grinning at him. "I haven't heard you laugh like that in a while."

"I decided to change my attitude," Gerald said. "What's the worst thing that could happen? Like your mother says, I have money. And options."

"It's good to be king, huh?" I deadpanned. "But I wouldn't be booking any flights just yet, Gerald. I know I'm right about this." I tucked Max against my chest then got to my feet. "Let's get you inside."

I gave her a quick sponge bath then rubbed lotion on her and slipped her into a fresh diaper. I placed her in the crib, spent a few minutes watching until I was sure she was getting ready to drift off, then showered and changed. When I returned fifteen minutes later, Max was sound asleep, and I headed for the living room where the gang was trying to decide what to watch. I grabbed my phone and headed outside to the patio where the dogs were sacked out under the overhead misting system. Chloe raised her head when she heard me coming, but didn't have the energy to get up. She thumped her tail a few times then closed her eyes and went back to sleep.

I thought about reading, decided against it, then stretched out on a lounge chair near the dogs and closed my eyes, enjoying the onshore breeze that was freshening. I was just about to doze off when my phone chirped, and I bolted upright to answer it.

"This is Suzy."

"It's me," Agent Tompkins said.

"Hey. Thanks for calling, Agent Tompkins," I said, taking a few deep breaths. "You must have something to tell me."

"I do," he said. "How would you like to come work for me?"

"Thanks, but I'll pass. It's not Quiver, is it?"

"No, it's not."

I let out a screech that scared the crap out of the dogs and probably everyone inside the house.

"You're positive?"

"We are," Agent Tompkins said.

"What's the matter, darling?" my mother said, poking her head outside.

"I was right," I said. "It's not Little Billy."

"Son of a gun," Gerald said, his head towering over my mother's in the doorway.

Moments later, Josie and Chef Claire joined the onlookers, and all four remained inside but with their necks craned to better hear my side of the conversation.

"I don't know how you did it, Suzy," Agent Tompkins said. "But I am really, really impressed."

"Thanks, Agent Tompkins. That's sweet of you to say. Who's the guy?"

"We have no idea. Whoever it is, isn't in our database," he said. "It turns out the guy was fifty-percent human, fifty-percent Newfie."

"What?"

He remained quiet for several moments. Eventually, I nudged the conversation forward.

"Uh, Agent Tompkins?"

"It was a joke, Suzy."

"Oh. Good one, Agent Tompkins," I said, then a question floated to the surface. "Can you guys even test for dog DNA?"

"I'm sure we can, but we didn't," he said, laughing.

"Wow. Gamechanger."

"It certainly is," he said. "Now, the next thing is to figure out a way to get our hands on Mr. Quiver."

"Has he landed yet?"

"He has. His sailboat's anchored off Havana."

"What about the Weimaraner?"

"She's with Quiver. Safe and sound," Agent Tompkins said. "One of our guys picked up his trail when he hit shore and followed him. He spent last night drinking at a local bar. According to the agent, he was greeted like a regular when he walked in. It probably didn't hurt he bought drinks for everybody all night."

"So, he's spent some time down there."

"Enough to have a favorite local," he said.

"That might come in handy," I said, giving it some thought.

"Why's that?"

"Hang on," I said, then put my hand over the phone and called out to Gerald. "You got a minute?"

Gerald strolled onto the patio and sat down across from me.

"I'm going to put you on speaker," I said to Agent Tompkins.

"Who's there?" he said, a cautious tone creeping into his voice.

"Gerald."

"Okay. Hello, Premier," Agent Tompkins said. "How are you doing?"

"I think I'm about to get a whole lot better," Gerald said. "It's nice to finally talk to you. Suzy's told me a lot."

"Unfortunately, there's not much I can do about that," the FBI agent deadpanned. "Even the FBI's power has limits."

"Funny," I said, trying to organize my thoughts. "Did you guys get a chance to look into Quiver's foundation?"

"We did."

"And?"

"And you were right again."

"I was?" I said, surprised. "Wow. Maybe I should play the lottery this week."

"A week ago, he made a major withdrawal from the Quiver Society's primary account," Agent Tompkins said.

“He closed it out?” I said.

“No. He left a dollar in it.”

“Really?” I said, glancing at Gerald. “Nice touch.”

“Yeah, at least Little Billy hasn’t lost his sense of humor,” Gerald said.

“What’s that?” Agent Tompkins said.

“Nothing,” I said. “How much did he withdraw?”

“A little over four and a half million. And even if he had to pony up half of that to buy sanctuary, he’s still got more than enough.”

“Will you be able to extradite him?” Gerald said.

“One never knows with Cuba,” Agent Tompkins said. “And if he’s paid off the right people, I don’t like our chances.”

“It doesn’t matter,” I said. “He’s gonna come to us.”

“Is he now?” Agent Tompkins said with a chuckle. “And just how do you plan on making that happen, Suzy?”

“By tempting him. Quiver seems to be a fan of the personal note, so I think we should return the favor.”

“Right,” Gerald said, nodding. “The note.”

“What note?” Agent Tompkins snapped.

“Relax, Agent Tompkins,” I said. “It’s just an idea we’ve been kicking around.”

“Well, I’d love to hear it,” he said, then waited in silence.

I nodded at Gerald for him to take the lead. He leaned in close to the phone.

"I have some…contacts on the island," Gerald said. "And we, actually it was Suzy's idea, thought we could get a note to Quiver telling him I have his money and will turn it over if he's able to get me out of my current predicament."

"And how exactly would he be able to do that, Premier?" Agent Tompkins said. "From what I understand, the local cops have some pretty incriminating evidence against you."

"They do," Gerald said. "We're still working out some of the details."

"I see," the FBI agent said. "But if you're able to come up with something solid, you think you can get him to head back to Cayman?"

"It's fifty million, Agent Tompkins," I said. "Wouldn't that make you come back? You know, take a calculated risk for that much money?"

"It's definitely a nice chunk of change. This is the fifty million you and Bentley donated to build the hospital, right, Premier?"

"Yes, it was," Gerald said, glancing nervously at me.

"And that *fifty* million built a wonderful facility," I said, returning Gerald's stare. I lowered my voice to a whisper. "Relax. I'm not going to throw you under the bus. We'll talk about the two million later."

"You're breaking up," Agent Tompkins said. "What did you say?"

"I was just saying we all need to take a deep breath and relax. We're very close to getting this guy."

"How are you going to get the note to Quiver?" Agent Tompkins said.

"Well, we know he's a regular at that bar," I said. "Why don't we have Gerald's contact leave it with one of the bartenders to give to Quiver the next time he comes in?"

"That could work," Agent Tompkins said. "Can you trust this guy? I mean, can he be discrete?"

"That's one thing I always insist on," Gerald said.

"Yeah, I bet you do," Agent Tompkins said, his official FBI tone returning. "Okay, you get the note delivered, and I'll have our guys keep a close eye on the bar. We'll let you know when he picks it up."

"Thanks, Agent Tompkins."

"No, thank you, Suzy. Well done."

"It just sort of came to me," I said, shrugging it off.

"I wish it were a teachable skill," he said.

"Be careful what you wish for," I said, rubbing my forehead. "I'm not sure I'd recommend it to others."

"Okay, I need to run," Agent Tompkins said. "Keep me in the loop."

"Will do," I said, my headache worsening.

"Thank you, Agent Tompkins," Gerald said. "I owe you big time."

"You have no idea, Premier," the FBI agent said, laughing.

"I'm sorry," Gerald said, frowning. "I'm not following you."

"You will. It'll be perfectly clear the next time we come looking for...let's call it, one of your especially creative financial residents."

"I understand, Agent Tompkins," Gerald said. "I suppose I'll be able to help you out with that."

"Oh, you bet your ass, you will. Later."

He ended the call and Gerald shook his head.

"Out of the frying pan into the fire, huh?"

"Hey, you didn't think he was gonna do it for free, did you? We're talking about the FBI, Gerald."

"Yeah. And it still beats hiding out the rest of my life or going to prison," he said, getting to his feet.

"There you go. The glass is half-full," I said, heading inside. "If it comes to it, just give up one of your political enemies." I gently punched his shoulder. "You must have a long list to choose from."

"You're lucky you're cute," he said, playfully shoving me back.

"Aren't you sweet? C'mon, let's go do some creative writing."

Chapter 25

The next evening, we were in the middle of a film, a decent thriller that had taken me about forty-five minutes to piece together, when Gerald's phone buzzed. He checked the number and grunted.

"That was quick," he said, hopping up off the couch. "Hey, what have you got for me?"

Josie frowned at the interruption but put the movie on pause. She glanced at me.

"You already know who did it, don't you?"

"I do."

"Well, don't ruin it," she said.

I focused on Gerald who alternated between silent, rapt attention and short responses to what the caller was saying. He ended the call and sat back down.

"Quiver just picked up the note," Gerald said.

"Is he still at the bar?" I said, ignoring the dirty look Josie was giving me.

"Yeah. And he's hammered."

"Then I imagine he'll wait until morning to give you a call," I said.

"You're probably right," Gerald said. "And my guy said right after he read it, he bought a round of drinks on the house. He'll be seeing that fifty million in his sleep."

"It's nice to have a dream." Then my phone buzzed. "This is Suzy. Oh, hi. Hang on a sec." I turned to Josie. "I'm gonna take this outside and let you get back to your imaginary murder."

"Thank you," Josie said.

"Are you sure you don't want me to tell you who did it?"

"Shut it," everyone snapped.

"Okay, okay, cool your jets," I said, laughing as I headed outside to the patio. "Sorry about that, Agent Tompkins."

"No problem," he said. "Quiver just picked up the note."

"And bought a round of drinks on the house," I said.

"What?"

"Gerald's contact just called him," I said.

"I should have known you'd find out first. Has Quiver reached out to Gerald?"

"No, apparently he's hammered. Our guess is he'll call tomorrow."

"Makes sense. I'd want a clear head to have a fifty-million-dollar conversation."

"You think Quiver will sail back?" I said.

"No, he's going to want to get this over with. He'll fly back. Probably via charter. He wouldn't risk going commercial."

"So, we just need to sit back and wait, huh?"

"We?"

"Of course."

"I think we can handle it from here, Suzy," Agent Tompkins said.

"No, Josie and I need to be there," I said.

"Why on earth would you guys need to tag along?"

"To get the dog. What other reason would we have?"

He fell silent and I waited him out.

"Okay," he said. "But just to get the dog. And then the two of you will hit the road, right?"

"Sure, sure."

"Why do I suddenly have a bad feeling?"

"It's probably something you ate, Agent Tompkins."

"I'm signing off now. Talk with you soon."

"I'm looking forward to it," I said, then headed inside with an extra bounce in my step.

The gang was closely following the action scene playing out on screen and didn't even notice my presence. I motioned at Gerald and he followed me down the hall. I poked my head through my bedroom door and beamed at Max who was sound asleep on her back. Gerald peered at her over my shoulder and softly chuckled. I closed the door and leaned against the wall.

"She's something else," Gerald said.

"Yeah," I said, still smiling. "I think I'll keep her."

He stifled a laugh then sat down on the tile with his back against the wall. He looked comfortable, so I followed suit and slid down the wall directly across from him.

"Are you gonna be okay handling this?" I said.

"Well, I have to admit to being a bit nervous," Gerald said. "Little Billy's already killed two people that we know of. Who knows how many more he's killed, or had killed, over the years?"

"According to Paulie, lots."

"How do you think he's going to want to handle it?"

"Well, I imagine he'll want to meet somewhere he feels safe," I said, mulling it over. "He's going to be on the lookout for signs he's being set up. Maybe near the airport in case he decides he needs to make a quick getaway."

"Yeah, maybe," Gerald said, deep in thought.

"No, now that I think about it, that's not it," I said, shaking my head. "It's too risky. A plane, even a private one, would be easy to track."

"Maybe he's got another location in mind that doesn't have extradition," Gerald said. "As long as he could land safely, nobody would be able to touch him once he's on the ground."

"You're right," I said, then shook my head again. "No, I don't like it. I think he's going to want to do it out on the water."

"Why's that?"

"Well, he'll probably want to do it after the sun goes down. And being on the water at night gives him a lot of flexibility. Especially if he's got the right boat. Or boats."

"I'm not following you, Suzy."

"Yeah, sorry about that. I'm kind of spitballing my way through this," I said, grinning at him. "But he's a sailor. That means he's comfortable being out at sea. And Quiver's spent time down here. So, he probably knows his way around the local waters."

"Okay," Gerald said, frowning. "But I still don't know what you're getting at."

"Oh, you caught that," I deadpanned. "This is a tricky one. How would you handle it if you were Quiver?"

Gerald vigorously scratched the back of his head as he gave the question some serious thought.

"Fleas?"

"Don't start," he said with a frown. "Well, he's definitely going to be on the lookout for the possibility I'm trying to set him up."

"He will," I said. "That's why you need to convince him how scared you are when he calls. Really play it up about how worried you are that you're going to have to resign. And maybe go to prison."

"That won't be hard to pull off."

"Relax, Gerald. We're in the home stretch."

"I want to believe you," he said, forcing a laugh. "He must know that the FBI is looking for him, right?"

"*Was* looking for him," I said. "Make sure you emphasize the fact that everybody, including the cops, thinks he's dead."

"Okay," he said, his expression again morphing into a deep frown. "But that raises another question."

"What's that?"

"How did *I* know he was still alive?"

"Oh, that's an easy one, Gerald."

"I'm glad you think so," he said, again scratching his head. "Because that one has been driving me nuts."

"You knew he was alive because you saw him," I said.

"I did?"

"Yes, from your rooftop terrace. Through your telescope. You were up there checking out the boats and topless sunbathers when you happened to spot his boat leaving the island."

"Son of a gun," Gerald said. "That'll work. I can even give him the exact time and date."

"Make sure you do just that," I said. "It's a good detail to toss out."

"I've got another question."

"Hey, you're kinda cutting into my territory, Gerald."

He began to laugh, and I held a finger to my lips and pointed at the bedroom where Max was sound asleep.

"Sorry," he whispered. "How do I convince Quiver I haven't called the cops?"

"You really need to ask me that question, Gerald?" I said, scowling at him.

"Yeah, Suzy," he said, making a face at me. "I think I do."

"Think about it."

He fell silent, then shook his head.

"I got nothing."

"Quiver's a criminal," I said. "Put yourself in his shoes. What's the one thing a criminal would never do if he had stolen fifty million bucks?"

"Got it," he said. "The last thing he'd do is call the cops."

"From Quiver's perspective, you're already on the hook for a murder charge. If it were to come out you killed somebody to hide the fact you'd stolen fifty million, you'd lose a lot more than just your title."

"It sounds really bad when you say it out loud."

"It is bad," I said. "Fortunately, it didn't happen. Apart from the two million you and Bentley kept for yourself."

"What about it?" he said, raising an eyebrow.

"You're gonna have to give it back," I said, making solid eye contact.

"What? No way, Suzy. Nobody has ever missed it. And hardly anybody even knows about it."

"I know about it."

"All of a sudden, you're turning self-righteous?"

"Call it what you want," I said, shrugging. "But you have to give it back."

He sat quietly, biting his tongue, I was sure, to stifle the response he was dying to give me.

"Sometimes, I wish you were more like your mother. She understands how things work down here."

"Oh, I've got a pretty good understanding of how things work, Gerald," I said, glaring at him. "I just don't like it. And my mother makes her own choices."

"I just can't write a check for two million dollars," he said. "That would raise a ton of questions."

"It would," I said, nodding. "But an anonymous gift to the hospital wouldn't."

"Damn you, Suzy," he said, shaking his head. "You certainly know how to kill the mood."

"You can afford it, Gerald."

"I can," he said with a shrug. "But it's gonna hurt."

"It's supposed to hurt," I said. "Clear your conscience."

"My conscience has been perfectly fine up to this point."

"Fair enough," I said. "Then let me rephrase. Stop taking stuff that doesn't belong to you."

"That was a long time ago, Suzy," he said, getting to his feet.

"Yeah, it was," I said, also standing. "But yet here we are dealing with it twenty years later. Are you familiar with the concept of Karma?"

"That's the name of an Indian curry, right?" he said with a grin.

"Yeah, close enough," I said, gently punching his shoulder as we headed back into the living room where the movie had just ended.

Josie spotted us and she focused on me.

"Okay, Smarty Pants," she said. "I just bet Chef Claire ten bucks you hadn't figured out who the killer was."

"You should stop throwing your money away, Josie," I said, winking at Chef Claire.

"Then who killed the heiress?" Josie said.

"Her lawyer," I said, then grinned at her crestfallen expression.

"How on earth did you know that?" Josie said, baffled as she handed Chef Claire a ten spot.

"Because Chef Claire and I watched it last month."

"Both of you really suck," Josie said, glaring back and forth at us.

"Hey, you wanted to bet me a hundred," Chef Claire said. "I let you off easy. Where are you going?"

"To the kitchen, where do you think I'm going?"

I glanced at Gerald, then at my mother and Paulie who shrugged back.

"Yeah," Gerald said. "I could eat."

Chapter 26

As expected, Little Billy Quiver called the next morning at eleven o'clock sharp. Gerald, behind the desk in our study, answered and immediately put the phone on speaker.

"Little Billy," Gerald chirped. "How the hell are you?"

"It's been a long time, Gerald," the voice said, sounding fatigued, probably hungover. "Have you got me on speaker?"

"I do," Gerald said. "But you can relax. I'm alone."

"Then why do you have me on speaker?"

"Because I'm eating a sandwich and need both hands."

"Must be one hell of a sandwich," Quiver said. "And for the record, nobody's called me Little Billy for about twenty years. So, let's go with William."

"Okay, William it is," Gerald said, shrugging at me. "How do you want to do this?"

"You have my old man's money?"

"If I didn't, we wouldn't be talking…William."

"Probably not," Quiver said, laughing. "You'd be on your way to jail."

"I suppose that's still a possibility," Gerald said.

"Not if you don't do anything stupid, Pre-meer. Oh, congratulations on all your career success. You surprised me."

"I surprised myself."

"I would have thought you'd have taken the fifty million and headed off to some tropical paradise."

"I already live in a tropical paradise," Gerald said, shaking his head.

"Fair enough," Quiver grunted. "So, let me get this straight. You took the fifty million and decided to just sit on it all this time?"

"Rainy day fund," Gerald said. "You know how that goes, William."

"Rainy day, huh? Positively torrential. It's just been sitting in an account down there drawing interest?"

"Pretty much," Gerald said.

"Good to hear. How much is in the account?"

"Just under seventy-five million," Gerald said. "It could have been more, but I've been very conservative. It's averaged two-percent growth per year."

"Seventy-five, huh?" Quiver said. "Works for me."

"And you want it all?"

"Of course, I want it all. But I need to know something before we start talking any specifics."

"Go right ahead," Gerald said.

"How did you figure it out? You know, that I was still alive."

"I saw you," Gerald said.

"Impossible. After I got out of that damn morgue, I kept a very low profile."

"I saw you and your dog on the boat the day you left the island," Gerald said.

"Where did you see me?" Quiver said, immediately suspicious.

"From my house."

"Your house must be half a mile from the water. How the hell did you see me from there?"

"I've got a telescope set up on my rooftop terrace," Gerald said. "You were clear as a bell."

"Rooftop telescope? What are you, some sort of perv?"

I stifled a laugh as Gerald's face reddened.

"I like to study the sky at night," Gerald said eventually.

"Whatever floats your boat, Gerald," Quiver said. "How did you know I was in Cuba?"

"Samantha told me."

"What?"

"Actually, she told me she was looking forward to visiting Cuba," Gerald said. "It wasn't until after she was found in the trunk of my car, and I saw you sailing away, I managed to connect the dots."

"You knew her?" Quiver said, surprised by the news.

"Yeah, I met her right after she arrived on the island. I ran into her one night, we had some drinks, then had a little fling. You know how that works."

I sat quietly, marveling at the way lies rolled effortlessly off his tongue. Then I remembered he'd been a politician for two decades and had mastered the craft as an essential part of his job. Or he'd always had the ability and just ended up in a profession where he could take full advantage of his skill set.

"Did she mention me?" Quiver said.

"No, she did say she had a boyfriend, but she wasn't sure if the relationship was going to go anywhere."

"Well, she was certainly right about that," Quiver said with a chuckle.

"She said he was incredibly smart, good looking, and a real man of character. I'm sure you can understand why you never crossed my mind at the time."

"Funny, Gerald. What about the cops?"

"What about them?" Gerald said. "Are you asking me if I've been talking to them?"

"That's a good place to start," Quiver said.

"And tell them what, William? That I'm being set up for murder by a guy looking for revenge because I stole fifty million of his old man's money?"

"That would be a tough sell, wouldn't it?" Quiver said, laughing loudly.

"Why did you wait so long to come looking for it?" Gerald said.

Since it was a question that was still bugging me, I leaned forward and propped my hands under my chin, listening intently.

"I never knew about it," Quiver said. "Can you believe that? My old man was sitting on fifty million bucks and never said a word. Who would do something like that?"

"Slash Quiver," Gerald whispered.

"Hey, don't be badmouthing my old man," Quiver snapped.

"Yeah, he was an absolute delight. So, how did you find out about it?"

"Well, after he died, I knew he must have some stuff laying around," Quiver said. "But I couldn't find anything. I'd pretty much given up. Then one day about a year ago, I was going through some old files of his I'd never gotten around to looking at, and there it was."

"The account information?"

"No, the key to a safety deposit box the old man had in New York," Quiver said. "I couldn't believe it when I opened it."

"And you headed straight down here?"

"I did," Quiver said. "And then I discovered there was one dollar in the account. Imagine my surprise."

"Okay," Gerald said. "But how did you know what happened to the money?"

"It didn't take a genius to figure out that someone who worked at the bank had to be involved. So, I finally managed to track down Bentley in Barbados. Let me tell you, it wasn't easy."

"And Bentley told you I was involved?" Gerald said.

"Eventually."

I gulped when I heard the matter-of-fact, dead tone of his voice.

"Then you shot him and figured out a way to pin it on me," Gerald said.

"Actually, that whole thing was another gift from the Gods," Quiver said. "I went to Barbados to hunt Bentley down, then learned you were there to give some sort of speech. And after I confronted Bentley and he spilled his guts about you, it was a no-brainer. I guess you just get lucky sometimes, huh?"

"Yeah, lucky you," Gerald said, scowling down at the phone.

"The guy tried to tell me you'd given the money to charity," Quiver said, laughing again. "Can you believe the guy actually thought I was going to buy that?"

"I imagine he thought it was worth a shot."

"Well, he was wrong," Quiver said.

"So, how do you want to do this, William?" Gerald said.

"Yeah, let's get down to business. Enough of this memory lane crap. Tomorrow night. I'll be offshore. I'll text you the coordinates about an hour before we're gonna meet."

"Okay," Gerald said. "How do you want it?"

"Well, I sure don't want seventy-five million in cash," he said, for some reason finding his own joke funny. "Just move the money into one of those special accounts you guys love to use and give me the information I'll need to access it. I'm sure I'll be able to handle it from there."

"That won't be a problem," Gerald said, then paused when he caught me waving at him. "Hang on a sec, William. I just spilled mustard on my shirt. I'll be right back." He placed a hand over the phone and stared at me.

"Ask him about the dog," I whispered as softly as I could manage.

"Okay, I'm back. Disaster averted," Gerald said. "Hey, are you bringing your dog with you?"

"Of course, I'm bringing Ruby. She goes everywhere with me," Quiver said. "Why do you want to know?"

"Uh," Gerald said, frowning as he looked across the desk at me.

I made a hand gesture, mimicking a dog biting my face. Eventually, Gerald got what I considered to be an impressive, impromptu charades effort.

"I'm afraid of dogs," Gerald said. "I got bit when I was a kid and never got over it."

"Well, you don't need to worry about Ruby. She's a sweetheart. But she's definitely the goofiest Weimaraner I've ever had. You should have seen her the other day staring into the water at a couple of dolphins that were following the boat. It was hysterical. I can't even come up with a word to describe it."

"The word you're looking for is whimsical," I blurted in a whisper, then kicked myself for the outburst.

"Who's that?" Quiver snapped, immediately on full alert.

“Oh, that’s my housekeeper,” Gerald said, giving me the death stare. “She’s in the other room fighting with my chef about something.”

“A housekeeper and a chef?” Quiver said. “You’ve done well for yourself, Gerald. And as long as you don’t do anything stupid tomorrow night, you should be able to hang onto all of it.”

“I can only hope,” Gerald said. “But it does raise another question.”

“What’s that?”

“We need someone to pin Samantha’s murder on,” Gerald said. “And Bentley’s as well if it comes to that.”

“Already got you covered, Gerald,” Quiver said.

“How’s that?”

“I’ve set up somebody else up to take the fall,” Quiver said.

“Really?”

“Yeah, the guy’s been working for me for years.”

“And you’re setting him up for murder?”

“Well, I never really liked the guy much. But don’t worry, I’ve got him wrapped up in a cocoon Houdini couldn’t get out of. Just get me my money, and you’ll be off the hook. And then that will be the last time either one of us speaks of this unfortunate incident. Am I making myself clear, Pre-meer?”

“Perfectly. But I’m not sure I can trust you, William,” Gerald said.

Quiver snorted into the phone.

“Trust. Such an outdated concept.”

"You got a better one?"

"Sure. It's called leverage. Right now, I've got most of it. But that can always change on a dime. So, consider our relationship going forward to be a children's teetertotter in perfect balance."

"Whatever you say, William."

"Yeah, that's what I thought you'd say. Keep that phone handy. I'll be in touch."

He ended the call and Gerald sighed as he put his phone away and sat back, slowly rocking in his chair.

"What a delightful creature," I said.

"It obviously runs in the family," Gerald said. "Okay, what now?"

"Well, we eat lunch. Then go for an afternoon swim. And we wait."

Chapter 27

Josie and I were playing with Max in my bedroom trying to tire her out and get her down for a nap. The dogs were hovering, doing their best to help, but all they seemed to be accomplishing was revving up her energy level. Josie ushered them out then closed the door behind them, and Max turned her attention to the bottle I was holding out. Soon, she was nestled against my chest, sucking contentedly with her eyes half-closed.

"What a great kid," Josie said, staring at the baby. "I can't wait to start teaching her a few things."

"I can."

"Hey, she's lucky to have an aunt like me," Josie said.

"I suppose she could have done a lot worse," I said, then turned serious. "You sure you want to tag along tonight?"

"I wouldn't miss it. I gotta meet this guy," she said.

"Really?"

"Yeah, his total lack of morals aside, you have to admit it was a brilliant plan."

"Not to mention the fact he's killed at least two people in the process," I said, peering down at Max.

"There is that," Josie said, following my eyes. "I think she's out."

"Yeah," I said, slowly getting up out of my chair and placing her in her crib.

I grabbed the bottle of milk and nodded at the door. We headed back into the living room where my mother was sitting by herself reading a magazine.

"Did you get her down?" she said, glancing up.

"Yeah, she'll be out for a while," I said, sitting down next to her. "Where's Paulie?"

"He said he had something to take care of," she said, turning her attention back to the magazine. "Oh, Chef Claire just called. They're on their way."

"I've never seen anybody volunteer that fast," Josie said, laughing.

"Yeah," I said. "Usually it's like prying teeth to get somebody to do an airport run."

"Just take it easy when they get here," my mother said. "She likes the guy. So, don't screw it up for her."

"You're taking all the fun out of it, Mrs. C."

"Just behave yourselves."

A few minutes later, Chef Claire entered from the patio, trailed by Agent Tompkins. He had his overnight bag draped over his shoulder and gave us a small wave as he looked around the house.

"Geez," he grunted. "No wonder you spend the winters down here. This place is amazing."

"Yeah, we like it," I said, getting up to give him a hug. "I'm glad you made it down."

"No way I was going to miss this one," he said.

"Let me take that," Chef Claire said, reaching for the agent's bag. "I'll show you your room in a bit."

"And which room would that be?" Josie said.

"Josie," my mother said, her voice rising. "Knock it off. It's nice to see you, Agent Tompkins."

"How are you doing, Mrs. C.?"

"Absolutely wonderful," my mother said. "At least I will be as soon as you deal with that monster."

"Oh, I like our chances," Agent Tompkins said, then spotted Gerald heading in our direction down the hall. The agent approached and extended his hand. "It's nice to finally meet you, Premier."

"Same to you," Gerald said, returning the handshake. "Thanks for coming down."

"Hey, who could resist the chance to put the final vestige of the Quiver family away for good? Are you ready to go?"

"I'm all set," Gerald said. "I just got off the phone with the bank."

"You actually set up an account?" I said, surprised.

"I did. Agent Tompkins thought we might need it at some point."

"How much did you put in it?" I said.

"A dollar," Gerald said with a grin.

"Nice touch."

We all paused when we heard the doorbell. Josie headed for the front door and reappeared a few moments later, trailed by Detective Renfro. Gerald handled the introductions and the two cops sized each other up briefly before Gerald motioned for all of us take a seat. We all focused on the FBI agent, apparently intuitively understanding he would take the lead.

"Okay," Agent Tompkins said as he pulled his phone from his pocket and began reading from the screen. "Quiver flew in on a private charter about an hour ago and headed straight for the boat he'll be using tonight."

"What kind of boat is it?" I said.

"A big powerboat. One of my guys checked the model out, and it has a top speed of eighty miles an hour."

"Just in case he needs to make a quick getaway?" Gerald said.

"Our guess is he'll have another one somewhere offshore," Agent Tompkins said. "He'll switch boats and then head off to who knows where."

"You don't think his plan is to go back to Cuba?" I said.

"Doubtful," the agent said. "The word is out he was there. He'll be looking for another soft spot to land."

"But he's gonna land hard, right?" Josie said.

"That's certainly the plan," Detective Renfro said, then focused on the FBI agent. "I'm still not sure about putting Suzy and Josie in danger."

"Not that again," I said, glaring at the detective. "We've been through that already."

"They'll be fine," Agent Tompkins said. "They'll be at least five hundred yards away. And as soon as we get our hands on Quiver, we'll call them on the radio to get the dog. Then they will leave the area immediately." He glanced back and forth at us to emphasize his point. "Isn't that right, ladies?"

"That's the plan," I said.

"Are you sure they'll be safe, Agent Tompkins?" my mother said.

"I'm positive."

"Show me where they'll be," she said.

Agent Tompkins removed what looked like an iPad from his bag and turned it on. While he waited for it to load, he took another look around the living room and shook his head. "Must be nice. Okay, here we go."

He placed the device on the coffee table in front of the couch, and we all hovered over it.

"This spot represents the coordinates Quiver sent Gerald," he said, then gently touched the screen in different spots as he continued. "We'll have our people, supported by the local police, in boats here, here, here, here, and here. Suzy and Josie's boat will be there." He touched the screen at a spot outside of the circle pattern he had created. "Before they could get to Quiver's boat, they have to get past at least two of ours. And I don't like their chances of being able to pull that off."

I stared down in disbelief at the device then glanced at Josie and pointed at it.

"Any questions before I go further?" Agent Tompkins said.

"Just one," I said. "That thing is so cool. Where do I get my hands on one of them?"

"You don't," the FBI agent said.

"You weren't taught to share your toys, Agent Tompkins?"

"Darling, please. Just follow instructions and stay out of the way until you're told to do otherwise, okay?"

"Sure, Mom," I said, surprised by the lack of resistance she was putting up. "Does anything about this seem strange to you?" I whispered to Josie.

"She's way too calm," Josie whispered back. "I guess she's comfortable with the fact we'll be half a mile away from the action."

"Yeah, maybe," I said. "Are you sure you're okay with this, Mom?"

"I'm fine, darling. As long as you do exactly what you're told, I'm sure you'll be fine. Unless you somehow manage to fall overboard."

"Okay," I said with a shrug.

"And if I can't trust the FBI and local authorities to keep you safe, what good are they, right?" she said, glancing back and forth at the two cops.

"Did you get a boat for me?" Gerald said.

"We did," Detective Renfro said. "We'll go through it with you when we get to the docks tonight."

"How many cops are you bringing?" I said.

"I'll have a dozen," Detective Renfro said.

"We'll have every agent who's assigned down here available," Agent Tompkins said.

"How many is that?" Gerald said.

"Wouldn't you like to know?" Agent Tompkins said with a laugh. "You'll see, Premier. But don't worry, it's more than enough."

"I still don't know why we just can't have one of my officers grab the dog and take it straight to the shelter," Detective Renfro said.

"Hey, none of you would even be here if it weren't for me," I snapped. "And I've seen the way some of the local cops treat animals."

"Still, it seems unnecessary," Detective Renfro said.

"It is," Agent Tompkins said. "But do you really want to have the debate with her?"

"No, not really," the detective said, conceding defeat.

Chapter 28

The boat we'd been given, a lumbering, flat-bottomed fishing boat equipped with a twenty-horsepower outboard from the prior century, sat bobbing in a gentle breeze. Josie adjusted the earpiece she was wearing then dug through her bag and removed a fresh pack of bite-sized. She expertly ripped it open with her teeth and held it out. I grabbed a small handful then got to work on the chocolate morsels.

"Could they have given us a worse boat?" Josie said with a laugh as she tapped the wooden side.

"I'm sure Agent Tompkins was behind it. Just to make sure we stayed out of the way. I could swim faster than this thing."

"And that's saying a lot," Josie deadpanned, then popped a bite-sized.

"Hey, my specialty is running," I said, then grinned at her.

"Well, let's hope we won't have to use either option."

"We'll be fine. Gerald's going to get the guy talking then the cops will swarm the boat."

"And if they start shooting at each other?" Josie said.

"We duck," I said, checking to make sure the volume on my earpiece was turned up. "It's awfully quiet."

I rummaged through my duffle bag and removed two sets of night vision binoculars and handed one to her. I scanned the open water, spotted the boats surrounding the high-end powerboat Quiver was on then focused on the boat Agent Tompkins was in with another agent.

"What do you think?" I said.

"About what?" Josie said, grabbing another small handful.

"Chef Claire and Agent Tompkins," I said, continuing to focus the glasses on the FBI agent. "He's like a puppy around her."

"I noticed. But it's a stretch. They both work incredible hours doing totally different things. And there'd be all that constant danger hanging over the relationship."

"You mean, the possibility he could get shot?"

"No, I was talking about the chance she could drop a case of pasta on her head," she said, frowning at me. "Of course, I was talking about him."

"Okay, okay, I got it," I said, glaring back at her. "Lighten up."

"Sorry. Tracking down killers always makes me edgy."

I scanned the water and eventually spotted what I was looking for. I pointed off the starboard side, and Josie followed my line of sight using her binoculars.

"Sure, they give him the nice boat," Josie said, laughing.

"Well, he is the Premier."

We watched Gerald's boat approach Quiver's that was anchored and gently bobbing in the water. Gerald tied his boat to the ladder at the stern and made the short climb. He stood still for several moments glancing around in various directions. It was a move, I assumed, designed to give all the cops a good look at him to confirm his arrival. Then a short man came into view from below deck and casually strolled to the back of the boat. He extended his hand and Gerald returned the handshake.

"You're looking well, Gerald," the man said.

"How's your volume?" I whispered to Josie who nodded then shushed me.

"You too, Little…sorry, William."

"I decided years ago I would never be given the respect I deserved if people kept calling me Little Billy," Quiver said.

"Makes sense," Gerald said, glancing around the boat. "You came alone. I'm surprised."

"No, I have someone with me," Quiver said. "You know, just in case. He's below deck at the moment, but he'll be up soon."

"Keep your eyes open for him," Agent Tompkins whispered to everyone wearing earpieces.

"Quiver brought one of his thugs along," I said.

"Well, we kinda figured he would," Josie said.

"The guy you brought along," Gerald said. "Is he the one you're going to pin this on?"

"No. Actually, the guy I brought with me is an old acquaintance," Quiver said. "Did you bring the account information?"

"I did," Gerald said, reaching into his shirt pocket and removing an envelope. "I imagine you'll want to check it."

"Actually, if you don't mind, I think I'll do that," Quiver said, then called out. "When you come up, bring my laptop with you." Then he had another thought. "Oh, and don't let Ruby out."

"As soon as he checks the account, that's when Agent Tompkins is going to make his move, right?" Josie said.

"That's the plan."

"Here he comes," Quiver said, doing a half-turn as a man's head emerged from below deck.

Simultaneously, my stomach did backflips, my head filled with rage, and my heart shattered into a thousand pieces.

"Oh, no," I whispered as tears filled my eyes.

"I don't believe it," Josie said. "I'm gonna rip his throat out."

"Get in line," I said, barely managing a weak whisper.

"Paulie?" Gerald said, stunned.

"Hello, Gerald," my mother's boyfriend said. "Surprised?"

"Yeah, let's go with surprised," Gerald said. "What on earth are you doing here?"

"I'm sure you can figure it out," Paulie said.

"So much for you being out of the business," Gerald said.

"I can't believe he could do that to her," I whispered, then brushed my tears away with my sleeve.

"It's the worst thing I've ever seen," Josie said.

"Actually, I recently decided to get back in," Paulie said.

"Right around the time you heard there were fifty-million bucks in play?" Gerald said.

"Seventy-five," Quiver said with a laugh. "Old habits die hard, Gerald. I couldn't believe my luck when Paulie called me and said he was thinking about getting back in."

"But why would you do this, Paulie?" Gerald said, his voice shaking.

"Money," he said. "And I kinda miss the action."

"I never picked up on it," Gerald said. "You seem perfectly content with your current situation."

"Content is just another word for bored," Paulie said with a shrug.

"But how could you do this to Maxine?"

"Yeah, Maxine," Paulie said softly. "I'm gonna miss her. Hopefully, at some point, she'll understand."

Josie snorted. "Good luck with that."

"Yeah, he's got no idea. He better have a good hiding spot picked out," I said.

"Don't do anything crazy," Agent Tompkins said through the earpiece. Then he continued after receiving no response. "Suzy, did you hear what I said?"

"Oh," I said, pressing the earpiece tight. "You were talking to me."

"Of course, I was talking to you," he said. "It's a bit of a curveball, but just let it play out."

"A bit of a curveball?" Josie said, frowning. "Yeah, and the Grand Canyon is a bit of a hole."

"Just sit tight," Agent Tompkins said. "Both of you. It's going to be fine."

I had no idea where the agent's optimism came from, but I kept my mouth closed and my eyes and ears wide open as I refocused on the boat.

"How much is he giving you?" Gerald said.

"Twenty percent," Paulie said.

"Fifteen million," Gerald said. "You do know that's pocket change to Maxine, don't you?"

"Of course, I do," Paulie said. "But this will be my money. I'm sure you can understand the difference."

"Despicable, Paulie," Gerald said, shaking his head. "I thought you were an honorable man."

"I tried to be, Gerald," Paulie said. "I really tried. But like the Quiver family, somehow it must be in the genes."

"That's the rationale I finally came to," Quiver said, nodding. "Once I did, life got so much easier." Then he clapped his hands once and grabbed the laptop from Paulie. He sat down on the bench seat that ran the length of the port side and turned the computer on. While he waited, he tore open the envelope Gerald had given him. Then he began typing.

"Here we go," Quiver said. "Account number. Check. Password. Accepted. Account balance." Then he looked up from the screen and glared at Gerald. "What the hell is going on?"

"What's the matter?" Gerald said.

"Is this some sort of joke? A dollar. One frigging dollar?"

"I have no idea what you're talking about," Gerald said, taking a step toward him. "There must be some sort of mistake."

"Stay right there," Quiver said, setting the laptop down and removing a pistol from his pocket. He slowly raised it and pointed it at Gerald's head.

"Now?" Detective Renfro said.

"No," Agent Tompkins said. "Hold your positions."

"What?" I said, way too loud.

"I said hold your positions," the agent commanded again.

"This is bad," Josie said.

"Nothing gets past you," I muttered.

"This is not the time, Suzy," Josie snapped.

"Take it easy, William," Gerald said, slowly raising his hands. "We can sort all this out."

"Where's my money, Gerald?" Quiver said, his voice low and threatening.

Gerald lowered his hands, pausing on the way down to vigorously run them through his hair.

"I'm waiting, Pre-meer."

"Bentley wasn't lying," Gerald said. "We gave it all to charity. To build a hospital."

"I don't believe you."

"No, it's true," Gerald said, staring at the pistol pointing right between his eyes. "Bentley and I came up with the idea as soon as we learned how your old man was making his money."

"Why on earth did you care?" Quiver said.

"I still had a conscience in those days," Gerald said. "And the more time passed, since nobody ever came looking for it, I pretty much forgot all about it. Until I got your note."

"Damn you, Gerald," Quiver snapped.

"And after you killed Samantha, and stuffed her in my trunk, I panicked. Then when the cops found the murder weapon, and the news about Bentley, the thought of jail. All of it sent me off the deep end."

"So, you thought you could lie your way out of it?" Quiver said.

"I thought I could lie my way into a meeting," Gerald said. "And I was willing to take my chances with you one on one. I was hoping you'd come alone."

"You guessed wrong," Paulie said, then turned to Quiver. "What do you want to do with him?"

"I'm gonna shoot him, what else?" Quiver said, pressing the pistol against Gerald's forehead.

"No, let me do it," Paulie said. "You've done enough killing lately. Maybe you shouldn't press your luck."

"Yeah, you might be right," Quiver said, relaxing a bit.

"You know, first Bentley, then the medical officer," Paulie said.

"I almost felt bad about killing her," Quiver said. "But duty calls, right?"

"Paulie, please. This is not you. I'm begging you," Gerald said.

"It's gonna be my pleasure, Gerald," Paulie said coldly. "Consider it retribution for all those boring golf stories you love to tell." He looked over at Quiver. "It's okay. You can put that away. I've got this."

Quiver gave it some thought, then nodded and slipped the pistol back into his pocket.

"Thanks, Paulie," he said. "You're a gem."

"More like a millstone, Little Billy," Paulie said, pressing his gun against Quiver's temple. "You forgot rule number one, never trust a criminal."

"Son of a gun," I said, giving Josie a wide-eyed, open-mouthed stare. "It was a setup."

"Now, that was something special," Josie said. "I knew Paulie wouldn't do that."

"Right," I said, gently punching her on the shoulder.

"You completely fell for it."

"Did not," I said, lying through my teeth.

"Go get him," Agent Tompkins said.

Immediately, the surrounding waters were filled with lights and sirens as the boats converged on Quiver's.

"Okay, guys," Gerald said. "You can come get the dog now."

"The dog? What about the dog?" Quiver said, keeping one eye on the gun barrel pressed against his head.

"Don't worry, Little Billy," Paulie said. "She'll be going to a very good home. And I doubt if they'd let you bring her with you where you're going."

"I will pay you back for this, Paulie," Quiver said. "You do know that, don't you?"

"It comes with the territory, right? I'll take my chances."

"Mark my words," Quiver snapped, then focused on Gerald who was standing nearby. "Did you really give all the money away to build a hospital?"

"Yeah," Gerald said. "It's a great facility. Your old man would like it."

"Somehow I doubt that," Quiver said.

"Maybe I should shoot him in the leg so he can find out for himself just how good it is," Paulie said.

"Oh, let's not ruin the moment, Paulie," Agent Tompkins said as he climbed aboard. "But it is tempting. Well done, gentlemen. Well done, indeed." He turned and flashed a big smile. "Good evening, Mr. Quiver."

"Who are you?"

"I'm Agent Tompkins with the FBI. And this is Detective Renfro from the local authorities. Those folks out there in the boats are other FBI agents and Grand Cayman cops. And this," he said, holding up what looked like a cellphone, "is a recording device that has been working overtime the past fifteen minutes capturing every word that was said on this boat."

"Great," Quiver said.

"Would you like to hear a couple of snippets?" Agent Tompkins said. "Maybe the part about extortion and money laundering. I suppose we could throw in a kidnapping charge just for the hell of it. Or maybe you'd like to hear the bit where you confessed to double murder. What would you like, Little Billy? It's your call."

"What I'd like is to see my lawyer."

Detective Renfro snapped handcuffs on him and led him to the stern then helped him down the ladder. We stood on the boat and waited until they were in the police boat. I was about to start my climb up when Quiver called out.

"Are you the ones who are taking my Ruby?"

"We are," I said, pausing on the bottom rung.

"You will take good care of her, won't you?"

"Mr. Quiver," I said, as politely as I could manage. "You have a lot of things to worry about at the moment. But you can trust me, that is one thing you do not have to worry about."

We climbed aboard and I headed straight for Paulie and Gerald. I eyed both of them suspiciously, and they returned my stare with big grins.

"Something on your mind, Suzy?" Gerald said.

"You were in on this the whole time?"

"Of course. It was brilliant, wouldn't you say?" Gerald said. "And if I may toot our own horns, acted out to perfection."

"You were both great," I said. "You had Josie completely fooled."

"Excuse me?" she said.

"Yeah," I said with a shrug. "You might have had me fooled, too."

"That was certainly the plan," Paulie said.

"When my mother finds out what you did, she's gonna kill you."

"Oh, I doubt that," Paulie said.

"Why's that?" I said, raising an eyebrow at him.

"Because it was her idea," Paulie said.

"What?"

"She wanted someone on the boat who she completely trusts with your life," Paulie said. "Both of your lives. And Gerald's as well."

"Not that you were going to get within five hundred yards of this boat," Gerald said.

"Right," I said, scoffing at the comment.

"I'm afraid I would have insisted," Agent Tompkins said.

"How would you have stopped us?" I said.

"Well, we probably would have started by shooting a few holes in the wooden boat you were in," Agent Tompkins said.

"Okay, I've had all the intrigue I can handle," Josie said, then headed off. "I'm going to go get the dog."

"A couple of dozen cops and FBI agents weren't enough for her?" I said, glancing back and forth at Gerald and Paulie.

"She needed more," Paulie said.

"Like what?"

"Leverage," Gerald said.

"Leverage?" I said, even more confused.

"Yes, she wanted a bit more control over the situation," Paulie said.

"I'm not following," I said.

"She doesn't sleep with them," Paulie said, laughing as he pointed around at several cops who were examining the boat.

"Got it," I said. "I imagine you've had some interesting pillow talk the past few days."

"You have no idea," Paulie said.

Josie led the Weimaraner up the small flight of steps that led to the deck then let go of the dog's collar. She immediately began dashing back and forth, checking out the new arrivals, while surveying the boat for signs of her owner.

"She's looking for Quiver," I said.

"Yeah, she's gonna miss him for a while," Josie said. "It's too bad. A complete monster who also happened to be a dog lover."

"A redeeming quality?" I said.

"Nah, not even close," Josie said. "But we know the perfect home to help her start rebuilding, right?"

"We certainly do."

We both watched the Weimaraner go through her paces, at times forceful, others tentative and halting.

"She is a bit of a goofball, isn't she?" Josie said.

"Yeah, but it works for her," I said, admiring the Weimaraner. I looked at Gerald who seemed to be at peace for the first time in days. "So, I guess you'll be moving out."

"I will," he said. "I think I'll miss it."

"You know where to find us," Josie said. "And I think we should have a little send-off for you tomorrow night. To celebrate your triumphant return to office."

"Sounds great. And that reminds me," Gerald said. "I owe a certain reporter a phone call."

"What do you think, Agent Tompkins? Can you stick around for another day and join us?"

"Actually, I could use a couple days off," he said, glancing around the deck. "Okay, I think they've got this under control. Let's get out of here. I prefer being on solid ground."

"Solid ground?" Josie said. "Well, I guess there's only one way to find out."

"What on earth are you talking about?" Agent Tompkins said.

"You just need to ask her if you guys are on solid ground," Josie said with a grin. "You'll never know unless you ask."

"You're such a pain in the neck sometimes, Josie," he said. "You do know you have a real gift for that, don't you?"

"I do," she said. "But it's not a gift, Agent Tompkins. It takes dedication to perfect one's craft in the ancient art of Babble-Banter."

"Babble-Banter?"

"Yes. You have no idea how much time and effort it takes."

"I could ballpark it," I deadpanned.

Josie stared at me, then pursed her lips and nodded.

"Since you did such a great job saving Gerald's butt, I'm gonna let you have that one."

Epilogue

I stretched out on my lounge chair and glanced around at the enormous crowd. I took a sip of wine then rested my glass on my stomach and stifled a yawn.

"Nice party, Mom," I said, reaching out to pat her hand. "And thanks for offering to have it at your place."

"My pleasure, darling. I figured you'd done more than enough. And thank you. You went way above and beyond the call of duty."

"Well, we all knew he didn't do it," I said with a shrug. "I still can't believe you set me up like that."

"It was for the best," my mother said. "I just wish I could have seen your face when you saw Paulie on the boat."

"Priceless is the word that comes to mind," Josie said from the comfort of her lounger.

"You're one to talk," I said. "Which color did you decide on?"

"The pink one," Josie said.

"Oh, I like it," I said, nodding my approval. "Good call. I wonder what's keeping them?"

"They'll be here, darling," my mother said, shaking her head as she glanced around the lawn and pool area. "Everybody else is."

"I told you not to let Gerald handle the invitations," I said. "I think the entire government is here."

I watched the catering crew my mother had hired bustle through the crowd then glanced at the four grills working overtime.

"It smells fantastic," I said.

"I'm starving," Josie said.

"Stop the presses," I said, rolling my eyes as I looked at my mom who was laughing.

"Speaking of the press," my mother said, nodding at the reporter, Geoffrey Jones, who was chatting with Gerald near the pool. "Did you get a chance to read the article in today's paper?"

"I read it twice," I said.

"What did you think?" my mother said.

"Glowing is the word that comes to mind."

"Gerald's a hero," Josie said. "Where do you think his approval rating will be in a few days?"

"Ninety, maybe ninety-five percent," my mother said, then reached down to greet Queen who had left the house dogs for her usual spot. She lifted the dog onto her lap, and Queen sat perched on her stomach surveying the crowd before settling down. My mother gently stroked her ears and waved to Marjorie, Gerald's executive assistant, who had arrived.

"Geoffrey did a great job with the article," I said.

"He did," my mother said, waving to another group of people. "But how hard could it have been to write that one?

Gerald's anonymous gift of fifty million of illegal heroin money to build a hospital twenty years ago, capped off by him putting his own personal safety aside to play a major role in the capture of a killer. I'm sorry you didn't get any credit, darling."

"Don't worry about that, Mom. He needed all the good publicity he could get. I'm more than happy for him to get all the accolades."

"I know you are, darling," she said, patting my leg. "And that's what makes you so special."

"I thought the accompanying sidebar article was pretty interesting," Josie said.

"Indeed," my mother said. "An anonymous gift of two million bucks to the hospital."

"The timing is interesting," Josie said, glancing over at me. "You wouldn't happen to know anything about that, would you?"

"I might have mentioned something to him in passing," I said with a shrug.

"Yeah, I bet you did," Josie said with a chuckle.

"I suppose I should feel bad about putting pressure on him to do it," I said. "But I don't."

"Don't worry about it, darling," my mother said as she got to her feet. "He can afford it."

"Where are you going?" I said.

"I'm going to go check on my granddaughter then make the rounds and say hi to some of our guests."

"She's out like a light, Mom."

"I know," she said, beaming at me. "I just like looking at her."

She tucked Queen under her arm as she headed off with a wave and made her way across the lawn toward the house.

"Did you call the Inn today?" I said to Josie.

"Yup. It's so cold, everybody is pretty much hunkered down. But everyone's fine. And they all say hi."

"Well, I hope it warms up before we head back," I said.

"Warm is a relative term," Josie said.

"I was talking about higher than zero," I said, with a laugh then waved when I spotted Teresa and Rocco and her daughters heading our way. "Here we go. This is gonna be great."

"Hi, guys," Josie said. "You made it."

"We did," Teresa said, glancing around. "My, did your mother invite the entire island?"

"Hi, girls," I said.

"Hi, Suzy. Hi, Josie," the two girls said almost in unison. "Mom, can we go play with the dogs?"

"Hang on a sec, girls," I said. "Actually, before you do that, you need to go look in the garage."

"Oh, that's right," Josie said, playing along. She winked at Rocco and Teresa. "Somebody left a present for you here."

"A present?" the younger daughter said, glancing at her sister. "What sort of present?"

"Well, you're going to have to go and see for yourself, aren't you?" I said.

The girls grinned at each other then looked at their mother.

"Is it okay, Mom?" the older daughter said.

"Sure," she said.

"How are we going to know what it is?" the younger girl said.

"Oh, you'll know," Josie said. "It's got a big pink bow on it."

"Cool," the younger girl said.

Then they both took off and sprinted toward the garage. Teresa watched them go then focused on us.

"Thanks for doing this," she said.

"Don't mention it. You're doing us the favor," I said.

Moments later, all the guests turned toward the garage when they heard the loud squeals of two young, teenage girls.

"I think they like it," Josie said, laughing.

They soon emerged from the garage led by the Weimaraner who was still wearing the pink bow attached to her collar. At first, the dog was rattled by the large crowd, but then spotted our house dogs and headed straight for them, closely trailed by the girls.

"Great looking dog," Rocco said. "Thanks, guys. They've been driving us nuts about getting one. You know, one they could call their own.

"They're gonna do great with her," Josie said, watching all five dogs play and roll around on the lawn. "Ruby might be a little disoriented for a few days, but she'll settle down."

"What is she doing?" Rocco said, frowning as he watched the Weimaraner dash and bounce back and forth across a small patch of grass.

"It almost looks like some sort of dance move," Teresa said, studying the dog's movements.

"Yeah, she's a little goofy," Josie said. "But it seems to work for her."

"She's still young," I said. "She'll probably grow out of that."

"Well, thanks again, guys," Teresa said. "It was very sweet of you."

"You're more than welcome," Josie said.

"You ready to grab something to drink and make the rounds?" Rocco said.

"I am. Lead the way," Teresa said, draping an arm over his shoulder and giving him a peck on the cheek. "We'll see you guys in a bit."

They headed off and we sat quietly enjoying the evening air, cooled a bit by the breeze. We both spotted Chef Claire and Agent Tompkins chatting quietly by the pool.

"Did you talk to her today?" Josie said.

"You mean, about him?"

"Yeah."

"I did," I said.

"And?"

"He's been dropping hints about the possibility of her moving closer to D.C."

"What did she have to say?"

"Before or after she stopped laughing?" I said.

"Good for her," Josie said between sips of wine. "Why should she be the one who uproots her life, right?"

"Exactly. Especially for a guy she isn't even sure about," I said. "She likes him, but…"

"Yeah," she said. "And the last thing she needs is a disturbance in the force."

"Really? You're using a Star Wars reference?"

"An oldie, but a goodie."

"Actually, I think the phrase is a *disruption* in the force."

"Normally, I'd be happy to sit here and debate the point, but I'm dealing with a *disturbance* to the stomach at the moment. I'm gonna go see when dinner will be ready."

"May the force be with you," I said, then spotted Gerald standing by himself staring up at the night sky. I climbed out of my lounge chair and headed his way. "See anything interesting?"

"Hey," he said. "I was just checking out the stars."

"You really are a stargazer, huh?"

"Well, there aren't a lot of sunbathers around at night," he said with a grin. "I gotta have something to look at in the off hours, right?"

"You're a real piece of work, Gerald," I said, laughing.

"Thanks again, Suzy," he said, turning serious. "I am humbly and forever in your debt."

"Boy, I really like the sound of that," I said, laughing harder.

"Joke all you want. But I'm serious. Thank you."

I started to pull him in close for a long hug, but my sandal caught on a protruding tile, and we proceeded to lose our balance. We both staggered back a few steps, and I teetered on the edge of the pool before he finally managed to pull me upright, his hand firmly grasping the first thing it found. Which happened to be my butt. Embarrassed, he let go and shrugged at me.

"Sorry about that," he said. "That was an accident."

"Don't worry about it," I said, my face flushed red.

"But I must say, your new exercise program is certainly paying off," he said with a mischievous grin.

"Shut it," I said, adjusting my shorts back into place.

Then I spotted his assistant, Marjorie, staring at us from a nearby table. She leaned forward in her chair and said something I couldn't hear above the crowd.

"I'm sorry, Marjorie. I couldn't hear you. What did you say?" I said, sliding a step closer to her.

"Get a room."